LOVE'S CALL

LOVE'S MAGIC BOOK 5

BETTY MCLAIN

*This book is dedicated to all the ones
Who answer the call of
True Love.*

CHAPTER 1

$\mathcal{D}$ora Hawthorn entered the art gallery. A crowd of girls flocked in to look in the magic mirror display. Everyone wanted to find their true love, and the mirror claimed to show some women just that. There was quite a crowd, but it looked like the group had thinned since she was last here. She had been away at college, but she was home on break. She had not told anyone about the man she saw in the mirror when she was last home.

Dora looked around a bit, but when she saw the girls around the mirror leaving, she hurried over to investigate the magic glass. At first, it showed only Dora's reflection, then Dora's reflection faded, and she saw the same man she had seen before.

He looked a little rough, not at all what she was used to. He had on a long-sleeved flannel shirt and dungarees. He was wearing a black, cowboy-style hat, which he hung on the back of his chair before taking his seat.

He was in a café, sitting at a large table, surrounded by a large group of people. They had to be his family. The resemblance was amazing. A young boy called him Uncle Rafe, and he turned and grinned at the boy.

He glanced up, and when he turned back around, he saw Dora in the mirror looking at him. He returned her stare for a minute, then turned and looked behind him to see if anyone was there. Not seeing anyone, he turned back around and looked at the mirror. He glanced around, but no one was paying any attention to the mirror. He got out of his chair and started toward the mirror.

Someone called his name. He waved and said he would be back in a minute. He stopped in front of the mirror and stared into Dora's eyes.

"Who are you?" he asked.

"I'm Dora Hawthorn, and you are Rafe," she answered.

"Rafe Haggerty," said Rafe.

"Hi, Rafe," said Dora.

"Hi, Dora," said Rafe. "How can we see each other?"

"I'm looking in a magic mirror," said Dora. "It will show girls their true love."

"I don't believe in true love," said Rafe.

"I bet you don't believe in magic mirrors, either," said Dora.

"I think you must be my imagination," he replied.

"I'm sorry I bothered you," said Dora with a sniff as she started to turn away.

"Wait," said Rafe. Dora paused to see what he was going to say, but she kept her head turned away from him. "I'm sorry, Dora. I didn't mean to make you cry," said Rafe.

Dora sniffed again, and then she looked up at Rafe. "I don't know how the mirror does what it does, but I do know it works. I have seen the proof of it. Even my own Mom and Dad were matched by the mirror," said Dora.

"Hey, Uncle Rafe, why are you standing here talking to the mirror?' asked the young boy from Rafe's table.

Rafe glanced at him and then back at Dora.

"He can't see or hear me," said Dora. "Only you can."

Rafe turned back to the boy. "Go back to the table, Lars. I was just practicing the speech I have to give at the meeting. I'll be there in a minute," said Rafe.

When Lars was gone, Rafe turned back to the mirror. Dora was gone. The mirror showed only his reflection. He waited a minute, then turned and made his way back to his table.

All the while he was eating, he kept glancing at the mirror to see if Dora returned.

Dora wandered out of the gallery. She was distracted and not really paying attention.

"Hello, Dora."

Startled, Dora looked up at Moon Walking. "Hello, Moon Walking," she said. "I'm sorry, I wasn't paying attention. I did not see you."

Moon Walking nodded. She looked at Dora for a minute. Dora flushed. She hoped Moon Walking didn't know about the man in the mirror.

"When true love sends out a call, it must be answered, or it will fade. A person who does not answer the call may end up with second best. They will always have a blank place in their heart and soul that cannot be filled. Pay attention to true love's call, Dora. Talk to your father or mother. They can help."

After giving this advice, Moon Walking turned and went into the gallery.

Dora stood gazing after her. She closed her mouth and headed for the courthouse and her father. It was time to get help.

As Dora passed the ice cream parlor, she noticed a girl crying and looking down. Her ice cream cone lay on the ground. As Dora watched, a boy stepped into the ice cream and twisted his foot to smear it. The boy was laughing at the girl. The boy did not notice Dora coming over to them until she reached over and grabbed his ear tightly.

"Ouch," said the boy. He twisted his head slightly to stare up at Dora. "What you doing that for, Miss Dora?"

"Why are you smashing Cathy's ice cream and making her cry, Jimmy?'

"It was an accident, Miss Dora. I didn't mean to make her drop it."

Dora held onto his ear, and Jimmy squirmed under her stern look.

"Well, you can just go and get her another cone," said Dora.

"I don't have any money with me," mumbled Jimmy.

Dora let go of Jimmy's ear and reached into her pocket. She pulled out a five-dollar bill. "Take this and go inside and get Cathy a cone. Get one for you, too."

"Yes, Miss Dora." Jimmy took the money and entered the ice cream parlor.

Dora turned to Cathy. She had stopped crying, but she still looked upset. Dora leaned down and gave her a hug. "Don't let Jimmy upset you. I think he just hangs around you because he likes you."

"He has a funny way of showing it," said Cathy. Dora laughed softly, and Cathy joined in. Jimmy looked at them suspiciously when he came out with the ice cream and handed Cathy her cone.

"You know you are going to pay me back for that ice cream, Jimmy," said Dora. "I will expect you at my house bright and early tomorrow morning. If I'm not there, my mom will show you where the lawn mower is. I expect to see the front yard mowed."

Jimmy groaned. "You have a big yard, Miss Dora."

"Yes, I do," agreed Dora. "Don't make me have to come find you."

"I won't," agreed Jimmy. "I'll be there."

"You two run along and enjoy your ice cream."

"Thank you, Miss Dora," said Cathy and Jimmy as they went on their way.

Dora was watching them leave when a police car pulled up beside her and stopped. Dora looked over and grinned at Captain James Michaels and Officer Mark Black Feather.

"You handled those kids very well," remarked James.

"They are in my Sunday school class, the one I teach when I'm home. They are good kids. I have been worried about Cathy. I think her family is having a hard time of it right now. Her mother has been sick, and her father lost his job for missing too much work."

"Where did he work?" asked James.

"He was working at Lamar Industries," replied Dora.

"I'm going to have to look into Lamar Industries," said James.

"I wish someone would," said Dora. "They are not people-friendly."

"Give me Cathy's father's name, and I will get Cindy to talk to Angelica and see if she can help."

Dora wrote "Cathy Parks and father Malcolm" on a piece of paper and handed it to James. "Well, it was nice talking to you, but I am on my way to see the Judge. Tell Cindy I said hello."

"I will. Give the Judge my regards. I'll see you around."

The patrol car pulled away, and Dora once again headed for the courthouse. When Dora entered the courthouse, the first person she saw was the bailiff.

"Hello, Mr. Trenton, how are you today?" asked Dora.

"I'm doing good, Miss Dora. You here to see the Judge?" he asked.

"Yes, is he in his office?"

"Yes, he is. You go on back. He'll be glad to see you."

"Thanks, Mr. Trenton," she replied. Dora went on back to her father's office and knocked on the door.

"Come in," called her father.

"Hi, Dad, it's me, are you busy?" Dora said, sticking her head into the room.

"Never too busy for you," replied the Judge with a smile. Dora went over and gave her father a hug and a kiss on the cheek. "Now, what is this visit going to cost me?" asked the Judge with a twinkle in his eye.

Dora blushed. "Well, I have a couple of things I want to discuss with you. First is about Lamar Industries. They furnish houses for their employees.

But I know of at least two occasions when they have fired employees and thrown them out on the street with no place to go. They did not take into consideration the reasons for the employee's absences. One man's wife had just died, and when he returned from burying her, he was fired. Another one had a sick wife. He was trying to arrange care for her and two little girls when he was fired. He was thrown out and had to move in with his parents. They are all scrunched up together in a small three-bedroom house. There are two young brothers at home also. Do you know anyone at Lamar industries you could talk to? Maybe you could get them to lighten up on their employees."

"I know the owner. He doesn't live here. He has a manager in charge here. I will talk to him and see if he knows what's going on." The Judge took a pen and paper and made himself a note to check on Lamar Industries. "Now, what else did you want to talk to me about?" asked the Judge.

"Well, I saw Captain Michaels on the way here and he told me to give you his regards, and Moon Walking suggested I talk to you about something," said Dora.

"Moon Walking. Where did you run into her?"

"I bumped into her as I was coming out of the Gallery," answered Dora.

"Does this have something to do with the magic mirror?" asked the Judge with a wary smile.

"Yes, it does. I saw someone in the mirror."

"I see. Do you know who it was?"

"His name is Rafe Haggerty. I don't know where he lives. Moon Walking said you could help me find him." Dora looked pleadingly at the Judge.

The Judge studied her for a minute and then sighed. "Do you remember where we lived before we moved to Rolling Fork?" he asked.

"Not really. You moved here before I was born. I have heard you and Mom talking about moving here after Grandpa had his heart attack and about how Grandma moved in with her sister, since she didn't want to be alone after Grandpa died. You were living in Morristown, I think."

"Yes, we moved from Morristown. Rena and Blake were just toddlers. I was a partner in a law practice in Morristown. We came here to visit Grandma, and when I found there was a judgeship available, I applied for it. I got the job, so we moved here. I have never regretted it. This is a good town."

"What does this have to do with Rafe Haggerty?" asked Dora

"There is a Haggerty family who lives in Morristown. Your mother keeps in touch with Madeline Haggerty. They were friends. Amos Haggerty, the father, died five years ago in a logging accident. The family runs a logging crew. They also have a farm. It is mostly used to grow hay, but they do have a garden, a small orchard, and a few animals.

"They only had three boys when we lived there, but they later had another boy and two girls. The oldest boy, Frank, and his wife were killed in a car crash three years ago. Rafe is next in age and has taken over as head of the family. He is also raising Frank's two children. He has adopted them, but his mother helps him with them. Jason comes next. He is running the logging team. Liam just finished high school. He is going to start college in the fall. The two girls are still in high school. Your mother said Rafe had been dating someone, but when Rafe adopted Frank's kids, she took off. She said she was not going to raise a ready-made family. I think Rafe had a lucky escape."

Dora blinked at all the unexpected information. "I guess that is why Rafe was dressed in a long-sleeved flannel shirt and dungarees," she mumbled.

"Logging is a rough life. It is not exactly what I had in mind for you. You would be around a rough group of people," the Judge warned.

"Dad," said Dora impatiently. "I can take care of myself. You made sure all of us kids knew self-defense from a young age. I'm a black belt!" She had received her black belt in karate at the age of ten. She'd been girls' kickboxing champion for the state for three years, starting at the age of fourteen. Dora could out-shoot anyone around in target practice. "And I'm on my way to a good career, teaching. There is always need of teachers." She had finished high school a year early and was now ready to begin practice teaching. Then she could get her teacher's license and be a full-time teacher."

The Judge was nodding and agreeing with everything she was saying. "I know," he replied. "I am very proud of you and your brother and sisters. I just hate to see you move so far away."

"Rafe and I have not even met yet. Don't rush ahead. How far is it to Morristown?"

"It's about one hundred miles west of here," he replied.

Dora shook her head. "I am further away while I am in college. We all have to grow up, Dad."

"I know," said the Judge. "I just did not expect it to happen so fast." The Judge came around his desk and gave Dora a hug. "Go talk to your mother. She can fill you in on things I know nothing about," said the Judge with a twinkle in his eyes.

"Bye, Dad, see you tonight." Dora closed the door quietly behind her.

<h1 style="text-align:center">CHAPTER 2</h1>

*D*ora hurried home. She was anxious to talk to her mother. "Anybody home?" she called as she entered.

"Just me," answered Maddie, appearing from the direction of the kitchen.

"Where's Mom?" asked Dora.

"She had a meeting with the garden club," said Maddie. "Why, what's up?"

"I just want to talk to her about something," answered Dora.

Maddie gave her a questioning look and decided to drop the questions. "You want to go downstairs to the gym and spar a couple of rounds?" asked Maddie.

"Sure," Dora said, smiling. "Let me get changed and I will meet you down there."

The girls left to put on their exercise clothes. Their father had had the gym fixed up for them, and it was one of their favorite places to play while growing up. All four of the children spent many hours there. Their father and mother joined them at times. They worked with different trainers through the years for the different things they were interested in learning.

"What's it going to be today?" asked Maddie as she entered the gym.

"How about karate, we haven't practiced it in a while," answered Dora.

"Karate it is," agreed Maddie, coming to attention and bowing to Dora. Dora returned her bow, and the girls started circling each other.

They did their routines for about an hour before they heard their mother call from upstairs. They went up to join her. She glanced up at them when they entered the kitchen.

"I can see what you two have been up to," she said, smiling.

"Hi, Mom," said Dora, coming over and kissing her cheek. "Let me get a shower and change, and I'll help you fix dinner."

"Take your time," replied Lucy Hawthorn. "It's almost done. I had everything prepared ahead. All I have to do is heat it up."

"Okay, but I want to talk to you about something," replied Dora.

"Alright, dear, I'll be here," replied Lucy.

Dora and Maddie left to shower and change. Dora hurried so she could get downstairs and talk to her mother before Maddie returned. When she returned to the kitchen, she could see her mother had the food ready and was starting to put it on the table. Dora got the dishes and utensils and started to set the table.

Her mother looked at her and smiled. "What did you want to talk to me about?" she asked.

"I want to ask you about the Haggerty family in Morristown," said Dora.

"Why are you curious about the Haggerty family?" she asked. "You have never shown any interest in them before. I did not think you even knew their name."

"Dad told me to talk to you. He said you and Madeline Haggerty corresponded. Also Moon Walking told me to talk to you," continued Dora.

"Moon Walking?" She paused and looked thoughtful. "Is this about the mirror?"

"Yes." Dora nodded. "I saw Rafe Haggerty in the mirror."

"How do you know it was Rafe?" she asked.

"His nephew called him Uncle Rafe. When I talked to him, he told me his last name was Haggerty." Dora paused to decide what to say next. "They were at a café. There was a bunch of them around a large table. I saw him in the mirror, and he came over to the mirror and talked to me for a minute. Then the mirror faded back to being a regular mirror again."

Lucy Hawthorn smiled at her daughter. "What do you want to know? They are a fine family. They have had a rough time the last few years. First Amos, the father of the family, died in a logging accident. Then, Frank and his wife died in a car accident. Rafe has custody of their children. Madeline was glad when the girl Rafe had been seeing took off. Madeline didn't care for her. She told me she felt the girl looked down on the family. She never could understand why she hung around, but she was relieved when she left."

"I think I know why she hung around," said Dora with a grin. "Have you seen a picture of Rafe?"

Lucy laughed. "You may be right."

"Dad was worried about me moving to a town with a logging crew. He thought they might be too rough," Dora said.

"I don't think you have to worry about the logging crew. Rafe and Jason will keep them under control."

"What are you talking about?" asked Maddie entering the dining room.

"We were talking about Morristown," said Lucy.

"The town where your friend Madeline lives?" she asked. "The one you named me after," Maddie added.

"Yes," agreed Lucy.

"Why were you talking about Morristown?" she asked.

"Dora was thinking about applying for practice teaching there," said Lucy.

Dora grinned. It was genius. She could go to the town and meet everyone without Rafe thinking she was chasing him.

"You know, we didn't sell the Hawthorn house when we moved. Your dad let his aunt and uncle move in and live there. They have since passed away, but their granddaughter is still living there. If you decide to go, you can stay with her." Lucy looked at Dora as she passed on this information.

"Great, Mom! Could you call and ask her about me staying there? I don't want her to think I am trying to force her to take me in," said Dora.

"I'll be very diplomatic. She will probably be glad of the company," said Lucy. She perked up and looked toward the front of the house. "I just heard the front door. The Judge is home. Let's finish putting everything on the table."

They soon had everything ready and turned to greet the Judge when he joined them.

Lucy hurried around the table to give him a hug and a welcome kiss. The girls both grinned. They loved to see how much in love their parents were. Both girls greeted their Dad, and they all took their places around the table.

After everyone had settled, said the blessing, and begun their meal, Dora turned to her dad. "Mom told me about Hawthorn house in Morristown," said Dora. "She said you let your aunt and uncle move in there when you moved to Rolling Fork."

"Yes," replied the Judge. "She was my father's sister. Her husband was working as a mechanic. He did not make a lot of money, and they were struggling to raise their granddaughter. Their daughter died in childbirth, and her husband took off and left the baby for them to raise. I wanted to help. I told them they could live there, but I kept the title to the property. I didn't want to take a chance on her husband selling the house. He was a small-time gambler. I have my old law firm, Mills and Mills, in Morristown. The firm looks after the property and pays the taxes and insurance for me. I also set up an account at the local grocery for my aunt. They send the bill to the law firm each month. I left the account open for the granddaughter. I need to check on the granddaughter and see if she still needs help."

"I can check on it while I'm in Morristown," said Dora.

The Judge gave her a resigned look. "You are going to Morristown?" he asked.

"Yes, I thought I would go and check the place out this summer, as soon as I finish my last tests. If I like it there, I may apply for a student teaching job in the fall," replied Dora.

"Humm," said the Judge. "You mean you want to check Rafe Haggerty out." Dora smiled.

"Who's Rafe Haggerty?" asked Maggie. "Why would Dora want to check him out?"

"He is my friend Madeline's son. Dora saw his reflection in the mirror at the gallery," replied Lucy.

"Oh," said Maddie. "You really saw him in the mirror?"

"Yes," replied Dora.

"How exciting!" Maddie exclaimed.

"It is probably a good idea for you to visit and see more about the situation there before you do anything permanent," said the Judge.

"You are right, dear," said Lucy. "I'll give Sylvia a call and let her know Dora will be spending some time with her this summer."

"Thanks, Mom," said Dora.

"Can I go with Dora to visit Morristown this summer? I would love to visit and look around, and if I'm with Dora you two can go on the cruise you have been planning," Maddie looked at her mom and dad pleadingly.

Lucy looked at Dora enquiringly. "Do you mind, Dora?" she asked.

Dora smiled at Maddie. "I think it is a great idea. I am sure Maddie will be great to have along. Between the two of us, we ought to be able to handle anything that pops up."

The Judge sighed. "Now I'm losing two of my daughters to Morristown."

"You are not losing us, Dad. We are just going for a visit," said Dora.

The Judge just looked at her knowingly, but his phone rang, so he excused himself to go answer it.

"Oh, Mom, I forgot to tell you, Jimmy Banks is coming by in the morning to cut the front yard. I already gave him five dollars, but I am going to leave ten more on the table by the door for him. It is a tip for doing a good job. If I'm not here when he comes, will you see he gets it and get him a glass of lemonade?" asked Dora.

"Alright, what did Jimmy do to get on your radar?" asked Lucy.

"He made Cathy Parks drop her ice cream cone. I gave him money to buy more ice cream, and we came to an understanding," said Dora. All three ladies laughed at this understatement.

"Well," said the Judge, coming back into the room. "I just talked to Matthew Lamar. I called him earlier and told him about everything you told me. He has been checking into things. He has sent an investigator to Rolling Fork to see what is going on in the factory. He said he was going to have the two cases you told me about checked into. He will see both families compensated. He said he will let me know when he has any more information. He also said thanks for letting him know what was going on."

"I am so glad he is going to help," said Dora. "Thanks, Dad, for calling him."

"I'm glad you came to me. I know it seems like too little too late, but at least it will give the families a chance to rebuild some of the respect they lost and get on their feet again," said the Judge. "Anytime you girls hear of anything unusual happening in our town, please let me know."

"We will," agreed both girls.

CHAPTER 3

$\mathcal{D}$ora was up and sitting on the front porch swing when Jimmy came the next morning. He walked up to the porch shyly. "Hi, Miss Dora," he said.

"Hi, Jimmy. Are you ready to cut some grass?" she asked.

"Yes, Miss Dora," he replied.

Dora led the way to the garage and opened it so Jimmy could get the lawn mower. "The mower has already been filled with gas. It should be ready to go," said Dora.

Jimmy pulled the cord to crank the mower. Dora went back to the porch and sat down to watch. She had already brought out a thermos of lemonade and several large paper cups. She put the ten-dollar bill in her pocket to give to Jimmy when he finished.

She leaned back in the swing and gently moved back and forth. There was a gentle breeze blowing, and it was a beautiful day to sit and relax. She thought about Rafe. She could hardly wait for the next three weeks to pass. Then, she and Maddie could go to

Morristown. She was nervous about how Rafe would react when he saw her in Morristown. She hoped he wouldn't be upset with her. She sighed and swung back and forth as she watched Jimmy cut the grass.

When Jimmy finished cutting, Dora went and opened the door so he could put away the mower. "I have some lemonade on the porch. Come and drink a glass and cool off," Dora said, leading the way to the porch with Jimmy following. Jimmy sat down on the porch step. Dora poured Jimmy a glass of lemonade and watched as he drank it down.

"You did a very good job, Jimmy. Thank you. I have a tip for a job well done," said Dora. She took out the folded bill and handed it to Jimmy.

"You already paid me for cutting the yard," said Jimmy.

"I know, but you did really well, and we always tip for good work."

Jimmy took the money with a big grin. "Thanks, Miss Dora," he said.

"You are welcome, Jimmy. Take care, now, and you treat Cathy nice. Her family is having a rough time of it right now."

"I will, Miss Dora." With a wave, Jimmy hopped on his bike and left.

Dora laughed as she gathered up the lemonade and cups and went inside.

The next day, Dora and Maddie decided to stop by the gallery and look in the mirror. Maddie was curious to see what all the fuss was about. Dora wanted to get another look at Rafe. They entered the gallery and waved to Angelica, who was busy with a customer, and made their way over to the mirror.

There was one girl there looking in it, but she left with a disappointed look on her face.

Dora and Maddie moved in front of the mirror. Almost at once Rafe's image appeared in the mirror. He was combing his hair in what appeared to be his bedroom. He had his head turned slightly, talking to one of his brothers. It looked like a younger brother.

"Is that Rafe?" asked Maddie.

"You can see him?" asked Dora in astonishment.

"Yeah, who's the cute boy with him?" she asked.

"Oh, my goodness!" exclaimed Dora. "He must be your true love. You both have some more growing to do, but he must be the one meant for you."

Rafe started to turn toward the mirror as his brother started to leave the room.

"Hurry move back so he can't see you." She edged Maddie to the side before Liam caught a glimpse of her. "We don't need any more complications before we get to Morristown."

Rafe saw Dora looking at him and smiled.

"Hi," he said.

"Hi," she replied.

"I didn't know if I would see you again," said Rafe.

"The mirror shows what it wants to. I have no control over it," Dora said. "Was that your brother Liam?"

"Yes, how did you know his name?"

"My mother told me. She and your mother are friends. They have been corresponding for years," said Dora. "My family lived in Morristown at one time."

"Where do you live now?" asked Rafe.

"We live in Rolling Fork, but I'll only be here a

few more days. I have to return to college and take my final exams."

"What are you studying?" asked Rafe.

"Elementary education; I'm going to be a teacher," answered Dora.

"Who is that peeping around the mirror?" asked Rafe as he spotted Maddie.

"This is my sister, Maddie," said Dora. "She wanted to get a look at the mirror. We are shopping for birthday gifts for my older sister's little girl. She is going to be three in a few days."

"I have an adopted daughter." Rafe picked up a picture of a little girl and turned it so Dora could see it. "She's almost four."

Dora grinned at the picture of the smiling little girl. "She's adorable," said Dora. "With that grin, I bet she has you wrapped around her fingers."

"Yeah," agreed Rafe with a laugh.

The mirror started fading. Dora waved goodbye to Rafe. He touched his hand to his mirror, as if trying to hold on to the image.

Dora sighed and grabbed Maddie's hand and led her out of the gallery.

"You can't tell Mom or Dad about seeing Liam in the mirror. If you tell them, they won't let you go to Morristown with me this summer. Dad is already groaning about me seeing Rafe. If he finds out about you seeing Liam, he will go ballistic."

Maddie grinned. "I won't say a word. After all, we are too young to worry about it yet, but I can meet him and get my foot in the door."

"Let's go find Sissy a birthday gift. We can then start making plans for the summer."

The girls were in perfect accord as they

continued their shopping. They arrived home some time later, laden down with packages.

"Hi, Mom," greeted Dora.

She was getting ready to leave as they came in the door. "Hi, girls. From the look of all those packages, I would say you two had a productive morning." She laughed as she eyed their load.

"Well," said Dora. "We have a couple of birthday presents for Sissy and some clothes for the summer. After all, you can't expect us to go to Morristown wearing old clothes." Dora laughed at Maddie, and Maddie and Lucy laughed with her.

"Today is my day to help out at the soup kitchen, so I will see you girls later," said Lucy as she turned to leave.

"Bye, Mom," said both girls.

The girls hurried to Dora's room to wrap Sissy's presents and admire their purchases again.

Dora returned to college without seeing Rafe again. The time home sped by. Soon Dora was through with tests. She passed everything easily.

And so, she and Maddie were on their way to Morristown after many stern warnings from the Judge. Their car was packed with their luggage, sheets, blankets, pillows, and towels. They had no idea what to expect at Hawthorn house. Their mom had not been able to get in touch with their cousin Sylvia. Her phone was disconnected. So, they would have to see what was going on when they arrived in Morristown. They had the address programmed into their GPS and were ready to start this adventure.

When they arrived in Morristown, they drove slowly through town. They wanted to look around before heading for the house. It was just a small town, a lot like Rolling Fork, although Rolling Fork was larger.

They turned onto the street where Hawthorn house was. Dora parked on the street in front of the house. There was a large moving van parked in the drive. Two men came out carrying an antique sideboard from the dining room. Dora recognized it from pictures her mom had shown them while she was home on break.

Dora and Maddie got out of the car and hurried over to the movers. "I don't know what you think you are doing, but you can unload this truck and take everything back in the house," said Dora.

The men turned and looked at her. "Our boss sent us to pick up this load of furniture he bought from the owner of the house," said one of the men.

"Well, my dad owns this house and the furniture, and he has not sold anything in this house," replied Dora.

"What's going on?" asked a woman as she came out of the house.

"Who are you?" asked Dora.

"I'm Sylvia Deeton," she replied. "I live here. Who are you?"

"I'm Dora Hawthorn. My father owns this house. I don't know how you ended up here, but I'm sure my Dad didn't approve you moving in. Where's my cousin Sylvia Tibis?"

"Sylvia died three years ago. I was her nurse for nine months. She told me to treat the place like home."

"Does that include stripping and selling its contents?" asked Maddie.

"So, you didn't let anyone know about Sylvia's

death. You just continued to live here with my father paying for everything because he thought he was paying for my cousin," Dora added.

"Lady, we have to get moving," said one of the men.

"I told you to take everything back inside," said Dora.

"My boss has already paid her for this furniture," he said.

"Give him back his money," said Dora.

"No," said Sylvia. "You can't make me." She turned to head toward her car.

"You should not have said that," mumbled Maddie.

Dora turned and with a self-defense move threw Sylvia over her shoulder and onto the ground. She pulled her to her feet and pushed her over to the post on the porch.

"Maddie, give me your scarf and call 911," said Dora. She tied Sylvia securely to the post.

Maddie called 911 and reported an attempted theft at Hawthorn house.

The guys on the truck started to unload.

"Just hold it until the law gets here," said Dora, holding up her hand.

Just then the chief of police's car pulled up behind Dora's car and the police chief got out and came to join them. "Miss Dora and Miss Maddie, I presume," he said with a smile.

Dora smiled back. "The Judge called you," she said.

"Yep, he told me to look out for his daughters. I didn't expect to see you so soon," he replied. "What's going on?"

"Well, this woman has been living here in the Judge's house for three years without the Judge's permission. She did not let us know our cousin Sylvia had died. She just kept living off the arrangements the Judge made for his aunt and her granddaughter. Now she is stripping the house and selling the contents. I want her arrested and charged with theft and grand larceny. There may be more charges added later. Do you need to do anything with this furniture, or can they take it back inside?" asked Dora.

The chief looked in the truck. "Leave it where it is until I can get someone out to make a list and take pictures," he replied.

Dora turned to the men. "If your boss has bought anything else from this house, he will have to return it, or he's going to be charged with receiving stolen property." The man took out his phone to call his boss.

Two more police cars stopped in front of the house.

"I want to charge this woman with assault. She attacked me," said Sylvia.

"Lady," said Maddie. "If my sister wanted to hurt you, you would not be standing now. She only stopped you from leaving. You'd better thank your lucky stars she let you off easy. I would not have been so easy on you."

"What I would like to know is, where were Mills and Mills Law Firm all this time? They were supposed to be looking after things around here for the Judge," said Dora.

"Derrick Mills has been running things at the firm since his father had to retire because of illness. It's possible he was in on this woman's scam. I don't see how he could be unaware for three years," said one of the policemen.

"This just gets better and better," said Dora with a sigh.

Just then an elderly lady came out of the house. She looked startled to see all the police cars.

"What's going on, Stan?" she asked.

The chief turned Sylvia over to one of the officers to take in and turned to the lady.

"Hello, Mrs. Amory. I forgot about you living here." He turned to Dora. "Mrs. Amory has been renting a room from Sylvia for the last year and a half. She is a retired school teacher."

"Mrs. Amory, what did Sylvia tell you about selling all of the furniture?"

"She told me she was remodeling. Why are there policeman everywhere?" she asked.

"Mrs. Amory, I'm Dora Hawthorn. The woman who has been living here had no right to be in this house. She has been arrested."

Mrs. Amory turned very pale. She looked so faint Dora put an arm around her.

"Can I get you a drink of water?" she asked.

"No, thank you, dear," she said softly. "I just paid her my monthly rent. I do not have enough money to rent another place."

"You don't have to worry about it right now. You can stay here with me and Maddie for the time being. No one is going to make you homeless," said Dora.

Dora motioned for Maddie, and the two of them turned to take Mrs. Amory back inside and see what damage Sylvia had done.

Dora gasped when she looked around. There was very little furniture. It was mostly cheap stuff. All the antiques had been removed. The walls were bare where all the pictures and mirrors had been removed.

Dora took out her phone and called her brother.

"Hello, Blake, have Mom and Dad left?"

"Yes, they should be on the ship by now. Why?" he asked.

"Do you still have Dad's power of attorney?"

"Yes, what's wrong?"

"Everything here is a mess. Cousin Sylvia has been dead for three years. Another woman, also named Sylvia, has been living here spending Dad's money and selling everything in the house. I think the law firm may be in on it. I need you to get here as soon as you can," said Dora.

"Do you want me to see if I can catch Dad?"

"No, if we can't handle things, we will get a hold of him later," said Dora.

"Okay, I'm on my way," said Blake.

CHAPTER 4

"Okay," said Dora. "Blake is on his way. Mrs. Amory, Maddie and I are going to take a quick look around to see what we need to spend the night here. We must go by the bank and close the account my father set up for his aunt and her granddaughter. We also must close the account at the grocery store. I will let my brother handle Mills and Mills. We must get to the bank before it closes. Are you going to be all right?"

"I will be fine. I think I will lie down for a while," said Mrs. Amory.

After a quick look around, they found three bedrooms they could use without using the one Sylvia had been using. They were sparsely furnished but useable for the night. They went outside to unload their car so they could go to the bank and grocer.

When they started unloading, one of the police officers came over and offered to help. Maddie graciously accepted with a smile. When they started inside, another officer hurried to help. They soon had the car unloaded. Maddie gave the officers a smile and a nice "thank you." They smiled back, and the younger one turned slightly red.

They were soon in their car on their way to the bank. The girls decided to go there first because it closed earlier. When they entered the bank, there was a man in front of them. He had slightly ragged clothes and was limping. He had on a cap and had a scarf around his neck. Just a few steps inside the bank, he took his hand out of his pocket and held up a gun. In a shaky voice, he announced it was a holdup.

Dora had been watching him, but she was also keeping an eye on the security guard. When she saw the security, guard start to draw his gun, she side kicked the gun out of the man's hand, causing him to fall to the floor.

"Stay down," she told the man. She looked around at the surprised people and the security guard and shrugged. "It was not a real gun. It was only a toy."

"If you knew it was a toy, why did you kick it out of his hand?" asked Maddie.

"I wanted him down before the trigger-happy guard shot him," replied Dora grimly.

She reached down and pulled the guy to his feet.

"Why were you trying to rob the bank with a toy gun?" she asked.

"I didn't mean to," he stammered. "I felt it in my pocket, and I looked at the bank, and I was desperate to get some money to buy some food for my kids. They are so hungry. I haven't been able to find work since my accident. I just couldn't stand seeing them hungry anymore."

The man had silent tears running down his face.

Dora looked at the man, and then she looked around at all the well-dressed patrons at the bank.

"What kind of town is this? You have hungry children, and no one thought to take them some food?" she demanded angrily.

"How were we supposed to know they needed food?" demanded one well-dressed woman.

"If there is anything going on in town, there is always someone who knows about it, and they make sure everyone else knows. There is no excuse for letting children go hungry while you sit around with well-filled bellies," declared Dora angrily.

"The police are on their way," said the bank officer, coming over to Dora.

"You called the police?" said Dora.

"Yes," he replied. "He tried to rob the bank."

"You leave my father's account open and let a woman steal from him for three years, and you want to put this man in jail for trying to feed his hungry children?" demanded Dora.

"What are you talking about?" asked the puzzled bank officer.

"I'm Dora Hawthorn, and this is my sister Maddie. My father set up an account in your bank for his aunt and later her granddaughter. The granddaughter has been dead for three years, and no one told us about it. You just continued to hand out my father's money to a strange woman. I want that account frozen until further notice."

"Yes, I'll take care of it now." The banks officer went over a desk and gave instructions to the person sitting there.

Chief Welldon entered the bank. He took one look at Dora and Maddie and shook his head. "I can see you girls are going to shake things up around here," he said with a smile. "I can see why the Judge gave me advance warning of your arrival."

"We seemed to be in the middle of things," said Dora with a shrug.

"What's going on here, Harry Wells?" asked Chief Welldon, turning to the bank robber.

"This man tried to rob the bank," said the bank officer.

"He had a toy gun," said Dora. "He has a bunch of hungry children at home."

"We can't let everyone who's hungry rob the bank," explained Chief Welldon.

"You can release him into my custody. I'll be responsible for him," declared Dora.

"I can't do that," said the Chief.

"We will see about that," declared Dora, taking out her phone.

"Oh boy, she's calling her godfather," said Maddie, grinning, as they all listened to Dora's side of the conversation.

"Hello, this is Dora Hawthorn. Is the governor in? May I speak to him, please?" Hello, Nancy, this is Dora Hawthorn. Is Uncle Ralph busy? Could I speak with him, please? Hi, Uncle Ralph, how are you today? The Judge told you about that. You'll be the second one I'll tell right after Mom and Dad. Yes, I am calling about a situation in Morristown. I'm in a bank here, and a man named Harry Wells attempted to hold it up with a toy gun. He has a bunch of hungry children at home. It seems like everyone was turning a blind eye to the children going without food. Well, I was hoping you could send him a pardon and release him into my custody. I'll take care of everything. He wants your fax number," she said to the bank officer. The officer gave her the number and she gave it to the governor.

"Thanks, Uncle Ralph. As soon as I know anything, I promise to let you know." Dora turned as the fax machine came on. "The pardon should be coming through now," she said.

The bank officer took out the pardon from the governor's office and handed it to the chief. The chief looked it over and smiled. "You sure know how to get your point across. You now have custody of one Harry Wells and his family," he said.

"Let's go to the store and get some food for Harry's family," said Dora to Harry and Maddie. "Thanks, Chief."

As she started to leave, Dora turned to the bank officer. "Did you put a freeze on my father's account?"

"Yes, Miss Hawthorn," he said.

"Good," she said.

Dora, Maddie, Harry and Chief Welldon left the bank. Outside, Chief Welldon smiled at Dora and Maddie.

"Maybe I should just go with you girls. It could save time," he said, smiling at them.

"I think we can handle things for now," replied Dora. Maddie just smiled.

"Okay, you know my number if you need me," he said.

The girls waved goodbye, and putting Harry in the back seat, they entered their car for a trip to the grocery store.

"What was it you are supposed to let Uncle Ralph know about?" asked Maddie.

"Dad told him about the mirror. He wanted to be sure he got an invite to the wedding. I told him there was nothing planned yet, but I would let him know when something did happen," said Dora.

Dora and Maddie both laughed.

"Leave it to Dad to spread the word," said Maddie.

CHAPTER 5

They parked in front of the grocery store and entered.

"Take a buggy and start gathering some groceries. We don't need a lot. We will get some more tomorrow," Dora told Maddie. "I'm going to find the manager and get Dad's account closed."

Maddie and Harry got a buggy and started filling it. Dora went over to the service desk and asked to see the manager.

"What do you need? Maybe I can help you," said the clerk.

"My name is Dora Hawthorn. My father has an account in this store. He opened it for his aunt and her granddaughter. The aunt died some time ago, and I just found out my cousin died three years ago, and no one let us know. The store has been letting a strange woman charge groceries to my father's account for three years. The woman has been arrested, and I want this account closed until the case can be investigated."

All the time Dora had been talking, the clerk had been pulling up Judge Hawthorn's account on the computer. When she looked at the charges, she began to look a little sick. She did some typing on the account and then turned back to Dora.

"I have put a freeze on the account until further notice. Could I see some identification, please?" she asked.

Dora took out her wallet and showed her driver's license.

The clerk looked at the license and handed it back to Dora.

"If there is any way we can do to help with the investigation, let us know. We will cooperate fully," she said.

"Thank you," said Dora.

She went to find Maddie and Harry.

They checked out and started for the front door with their loaded buggy.

Dora turned her head to say something to Maddie and instead ran into someone coming in the door. The man caught her shoulders to keep from knocking her down. Dora turned back to see who she had run into and stopped still.

"Rafe," she whispered.

"Dora," he said softly.

"Hi, Rafe," she said, gazing into his eyes and smiling.

"Hi, Dora," he answered, gazing into her eyes and smiling back.

"You are here," he said.

"Yes, so are you," she replied.

"Hi," he said.

"Hi," she answered.

"We have already been through that," said an impatient voice behind Rafe.

Rafe moved over slightly without letting go of Dora and let his brother Jason enter the store. Neither of them paid any attention to the interruption. Jason started to say something else, when he glanced up and spotted Harry and Maddie.

"Harry!" he exclaimed. "I have been looking for you. You moved out of your house, and I could not find where you had moved to," he said, going over and clapping Harry on the shoulder.

"I didn't have the money to stay there. I had to find somewhere cheaper to live. I couldn't find work after I hurt my leg," said Harry.

"You got hurt on the job. You should have applied for workman's compensation. Your bills would all have been taken care of. You still have a job with us. We did not fire you. We would have found some easier work for you to do," said Jason

"I didn't know that," said Harry.

"Why don't you come with me and I will fix you up?" said Jason.

"I can't do that," said Harry. "I have to go with Miss Dora. She has custody of me."

"What!" Jason exclaimed. "How did she get custody of you?"

"She got custody to keep me from going to jail after I tried to rob the bank," said Harry.

"You tried to rob the bank," said Jason faintly.

"Yeah, with a toy gun," contributed Maddie.

"Who are you?" asked Jason.

"I'm Dora's sister, Maddie," said Maddie with a grin.

Jason glanced over at Rafe and Dora, who were still standing close, looking into each other's eyes.

"I take it they know each other," said Jason to Maddie.

Maddie grinned. "You might say that."

Dora rubbed her face against Rafe's hand on her shoulder. He rubbed one finger along her cheek. He started to pull her closer, but Jason interrupted.

"Rafe," he said.

"My brother Jason," said Rafe to Dora.

"Hello, Jason," said Dora

"Hello," said Jason. "Rafe, we need to go with them to take Harry's groceries home and see about helping him."

"Why don't you go and take care of him," suggested Rafe.

"Because he won't go with me, he said Dora got custody of him to keep him from going to jail for trying to rob the bank with a toy gun," said Jason.

Rafe grinned at Dora. "He tried to rob the bank with a toy gun?"

Dora nodded. "The bank wanted to put him in jail. He was just trying to get some money to feed his children. I couldn't let them put him in jail. His children need him," she replied.

"Of course, you couldn't," said Rafe. "How did you manage to get them to give you custody?" he asked.

"She called her godfather," replied Maddie with a grin.

"Your godfather?" inquired Rafe.

"Yes, the governor," replied Dora. "I have custody of Harry and his family. We are here getting them a few groceries."

Rafe looked at the buggy piled high with groceries and then pulled Dora into a hug. He laughed loudly.

"The governor. I love it. I'm so glad you are here," he declared, hugging her again. He turned to Jason, who had been a very interested observer. "Let's get Harry and his food home. The ladies are going to need help with all of those bags."

"Maddie, can you and Harry ride with Jason? Dora and I will go by a fast food place and pick up some food that is already cooked for tonight," said Rafe.

"Sure," said Maddie.

"Okay. Harry, how many children do you have?" asked Dora.

"I have five. There are three girls and two boys. The oldest is ten, and the youngest is three months," he replied.

Jason and Harry loaded the bags into the trunk of Dora's car. Jason was in a truck, and Maddie was afraid they might fall out of the back. Jason just grinned at her and let her have her way. He did not tell her he hauled things in the back of the truck all the time. Rafe watched and did not let go of Dora. Dora smiled. It seemed as if he was afraid she would disappear if he let go. She did not mind. She liked having him hold on to her.

Dora handed Rafe her keys, and he opened the passenger door for her to get in the car. When she was seated with her seatbelt on, he closed the door and went to get into the driver's seat. As soon as he had the car started, he reached over and took Dora's hand and put it under his on the wheel. They pulled out and headed for the local Burger King, with Jason following.

They decided to go inside to get the food. Jason, Maddie, and Harry all followed them inside to help carry the food. When Dora started to give them her card to pay for the food, Rafe took the card and handed it back to her.

"Our company owes Harry. We will take care of this. I want to reimburse you for that load of groceries, also," he said.

"We will talk about it later," said Dora.

"Just so there is a lot of later," said Rafe with a grin.

"There will be," replied Dora, smiling back.

When the order came—hamburgers, fries, chicken nuggets, and milkshakes for the kids—Jason, Harry, and Maddie loaded up. Dora only had one free hand. Rafe kept hold of the other one. They all loaded into their vehicles. Maddie joined Rafe and Dora so Jason would have room for the food. Jason led the way this time, with Harry telling him where to go.

They stopped in front of a run-down house in a bad location. When they stopped in front of the house, Dora sat forward in shock.

"What is going on?" she exclaimed as she hurriedly got out of the car.

There was a Child Protective Services car parked out front, and a woman exited the house pulling two children by their hands. The children were crying and trying to get away from her, and their mother was in the doorway with another child in her arms, begging the woman to stop. She had tears running down her face.

Dora ran over and got in front of the woman.

"What do you think you are doing?" asked Dora.

"This is none of your business. Get out of my way," replied the woman rudely.

"It most certainly is my business if you think you

are going anywhere with those children," declared Dora. "Now take your hands off of them and let them go to their mother."

"I had a report about hungry children here. When I checked on it, I found no food in the house, and it is not a fit place for them to be," she declared. "It is my duty to take them to a safe place."

"One of those busybodies from the bank is trying to cause trouble," Dora said to Maddie. Maddie nodded in agreement. "I have food for the children in my car, and I am about to move the whole family to a safer place," replied Dora.

"Who are you? Why do you think I will turn the children over to you?" demanded the woman.

"My name is Dora Hawthorn, and the governor gave me custody of this family. Do I need to call him so he can repeat his order verbally to you?" Dora took a paper out of her pocket and, unfolding it, showed it to the woman.

The woman turned pale and quickly released the children. When she turned them loose, they ran to their mother. "I'm sorry Miss Hawthorn. When I received a report, I had to check it out," she replied.

"I realize you had to check it out," said Dora. "Did it ever dawn on you to help this family to get on its feet, instead of breaking it up?"

"We have to do what our manager tells us to do. In this case, it would be to move the children," she replied.

Dora sighed. "I can see right now I am going to have a few words to say to your manager very soon," she said. The woman hurriedly got into her car and left.

Dora turned and saw that Maddie, Harry, Rafe

and Jason were handing out the food. Dora went over, got a hamburger out, and took it to the children's mother. She also handed Harry one. "Let's go inside and discuss what we are going to do now," she said. Rafe handed out food and watched with a proud smile on his face at Dora in action.

They all went inside. Dora looked around. She could see why the social worker wanted them out of this environment. She looked at Harry. "You know your family can't stay here," she said.

"Yes, I know," he said shamefully.

Dora went over and put a hand on his shoulder. "You did the best you could at the time. Now, it's time to accept help," she said. She looked at Jason. "If you can load their stuff into the back of your truck, it can be stored in my garage until we find them better accommodations," she said.

"Where will we stay?" asked Ruby, Harry's wife.

"You will stay at Hawthorn house. It may be a little crowded, but we will work it out," said Dora.

"Ruby, this is Dora Hawthorn. Dora, this is my wife Ruby. Dora has custody of us because I tried to rob the bank, and she wouldn't let them put me in jail," said Harry.

"You tried to rob the bank?" Ruby whispered faintly.

"I only had Lester's toy gun. I would not hurt anyone," replied Harry.

"Oh, my," said Ruby, hiding her face against the baby blanket.

"All right children," said Dora in her school teacher voice. "Each of you get a bag and put your toys in it to take with you. Ruby, you get what you need for the baby, you, and Harry. Also round up a change of clothes for the children."

She turned to find Jason, Rafe, and Harry already taking what furniture the family had out and loading it in the back of the truck.

"That's some lady you have there," Jason told Rafe, smiling.

Rafe smiled back. "She sure is," he agreed proudly.

"Where did you find her?" asked Jason.

"You wouldn't believe me if I told you," replied Rafe.

They headed back inside to get another load.

When they had the back of Jason's truck loaded, the guys came back inside.

"What now?" Rafe asked.

"You guys are going to take this load to Hawthorn house. My brother, Blake, should be there by now, and he can help unload. We don't have child seats, but we will just have to do without. We will get some tomorrow. Harry and Maddie can ride with Jason. Ruby and the children can crowd into my back seat. Have you all finished your hamburgers?" Dora asked.

"Are you kidding?" asked Maddie, laughing. "They inhaled them."

"Good," said Dora. "Let's load up."

Ruby and the children piled into the back of Dora's car. It was a tight fit, but they managed, even with each child holding a bag with their toys. Dora looked at the small bags of toys and shook her head. She and Maddie were going to have to go shopping for toys and clothes tomorrow, but right now they had to find them a place to sleep tonight.

When they were on their way to Hawthorn

house, Rafe looked at Dora and smiled. He had her hand under his on the wheel again.

"I think you should know," he said, "I was dating Sylvia Deeton, who lived in Hawthorn house, some time back."

Dora looked at him thoughtfully. "You had a lucky escape. Sylvia is in jail. She had no right to live in Hawthorn house. She has been robbing my Dad. I had her arrested this afternoon when I caught her selling the antiques out of the house. I caught the loading van and stopped them, but I am pretty sure this was not their first load."

"Wow," said Rafe. "I had no idea she was there illegally."

"I know. She had everyone fooled," said Dora. "I called my brother to come and handle the law firm. They were supposed to be watching the place for my Dad. I am pretty sure Derrick Mills was in on it with Sylvia."

"I would not be surprised. He has always been a bully and a sneak. He was in the same grade as Jason at school. Jason had a lot of trouble with him until I cornered him and threatened to beat the crap out of him if he messed with Jason again," said Rafe.

"You said a bad word," said a small voice from the back seat.

Rafe smiled. "I'm sorry. I'll have to watch my language around young ears. You would think I would have learned that by now."

Dora laughed with him. "We all have to learn that lesson," she agreed as they stopped in front of Hawthorn house.

CHAPTER 6

"*W*ell, the loading van is gone," said Dora. "I wonder what they did with the furniture."

They got out of the car and watched Jason pull into the driveway. Dora went over and opened the overhead garage door. The front door of the house opened, and Blake came out to join them. Dora and Maddie hurried over to give him a hug. They had not seen him for a while. They had already been on their way to Morristown when Blake returned home from college.

"I had a look around while I was waiting for you. There is a small apartment over the garage. It is in pretty good shape. I think I will take it. The movers took all of the furniture back inside and set it up after the police finished making a list and taking pictures."

Blake looked around at all the people. He grinned. "I see Dora has been busy," he said.

Dora grinned back at him. "I had to help. You know I cannot let children suffer," she said.

Both Blake and Maddie were grinning. Blake held

up a hand. "I know," he said and gave Dora a hug. "It's fine. Just tell me what you want me to do."

Jason and Rafe had been standing there smiling, watching the siblings' interaction. She reached for Rafe's hand. "This is Rafe Haggerty. Rafe, this is my brother, Blake." Dora pointed at Jason. "Jason is Rafe's brother, and the rest of the people here are the Wells family. Uncle Ralph gave me custody of them so I could help them and keep Harry out of jail for trying to rob the bank."

Blake smiled. "You got custody of a bank robber's family?" He didn't sound all that surprised. He held up his hand as both Dora and Maddie started to explain. "Tell me later. We need to get the truck unloaded and get everyone situated first."

The guys started unloading the truck, and Dora and Maddie herded the children and their mother inside. The inside looked much better with some of the furniture restored.

"Let Ruby and Harry have the room Sylvia was using. The baby can stay with them. There is a large walk-in closet in there. We can dump all her clothes into trash bags and put up a cot in there for Lester. The room next to them can be shared by the girls." Dora turned to Maddie when she finished talking. Maddie was nodding her agreement with the arrangements.

As Dora turned to Ruby, the guys came into the house. They had made quick work of the unloading. "Ruby, do you have any bottles and formula?" asked Dora

"I have a bottle, but no formula. I have been breastfeeding," she replied.

"We are going to have to get some formula. You

have not been eating enough, and you are dehydrated. You are not making enough milk. The baby is hungry. If he isn't taken care of quickly, he will end up in the hospital," said Dora. "Don't worry. We will take care of him." She put an arm around Ruby to comfort her as she started crying again. "Now, dry those tears. You are dehydrated enough."

"Jason, could I get you to take Maddie and Harry to the store to pick up some disposable diapers and some cans of baby formula?" she asked.

"Sure, is there anything else they need while we are out?" asked Jason.

"Probably, but we will make do until tomorrow," replied Dora with a sigh. She turned to Rafe and Blake. "Could you two guys see about unloading the groceries in the trunk of my car while I get Ruby and the children settled in their rooms?"

Rafe and Blake turned and headed to do her bidding. Dora picked up one of the smaller children and, taking another by the hand, led the way upstairs to the bedrooms. She showed the girls into their room first. It had a queen size bed and looked to be in pretty good shape now that the furniture had been restored to it. She led the way into the next room, which was the best room in the house. It had a king size bed and was well furnished. Ruby's eyes grew large as she looked around.

"You want us to stay here?" she asked.

"Yes," said Dora. "If you do not mind, my sister and I do not want to use this room."

"I don't mind. I have never stayed anywhere this nice," said Ruby.

Dora gave her a smile.

"If you can watch the kids, I will go and find some sheets and blankets and make up the beds," said Dora.

Dora went down the hall and found a linen closet. She pulled out a set of queen-size sheets and a set of king-size sheets. She grabbed pillow cases and a couple of blankets and headed for the girls' room. She put everything on a chair, stripped the bed, and remade it quickly. She pushed the old bedding in the hall to be collected later. She went into the master bedroom and quickly stripped and remade the bed in there. She then dumped the used bedding into the hall with the rest. She took the baby to hold and sat in the rocker to rock him while Ruby went into the attached bathroom to give the children a bath. Dora had dug up some t-shirts for them to sleep in.

She was rocking gently back and forth, humming to the baby, when Rafe entered the room looking for her. He smiled when he spotted her, and his expression softened when he saw her holding the baby. He came over and sat on a bench next to her chair. "Hi," he said quietly.

"Hi," she said just as softly. "Did you and Blake get the groceries put away?"

"Yes, Blake has taken some bedding and cleaning things up to the garage apartment. He wants to get it ready before night." Rafe reached out a finger and gently rubbed her cheek. "This has been quite a day," he remarked. "I have been thinking about you ever since I saw your reflection in the mirror. I am so glad you are here." He laughed softly. "I don't think Morristown is ever going to be the same again."

"Maybe it was time for a little shaking up," replied Dora. "I have been thinking about you, too. Mom suggested that I should stay the summer and maybe apply for student teaching for the fall semester. After I finish my student teaching, all I have to do is take the state exam and I will be a certified teacher," Dora stated proudly.

"Great," said Rafe. "I will be rooting for you, and I will not be far from your side. I want you to meet Dede and Lars."

"I can't wait to meet them. We all have to get to know each other," said Dora.

Rafe leaned forward and gently kissed her. He pulled back with a sigh. "I wanted to kiss you since I bumped into you at the grocery," he whispered.

"We have been rather busy. And the night is still young." Dora laughed softly.

Blake entered the room carrying an antique cradle. "I found this in the garage and cleaned it up. I thought the baby could use it temporarily," he said.

"Great," said Dora.

"I also found a cot and a gate to go at the top of the stairs. If you can help me, Rafe, we can find some tools and install the gate. We wouldn't want any of the little ones falling down the stairs in the middle of the night."

Rafe gave Dora's hand a squeeze and went to help Blake install the safety gate.

The children started coming out of the bathroom as they finished their baths and were dressed. They were losing some of their shyness and grinned at Dora. She smiled back at them and motioned them forward. She had them sit on the floor at her feet and asked them if they were hungry. They all shook their heads and grinned widely.

"How would you like a story?" she asked. The grins got wider and all heads were nodding. "Okay, story it is. Once upon a time there was this little girl. She had two sisters and a brother. Her dad was a famous judge. The judge was afraid the children would be in danger because of the bad people he had to send to jail, so he hired people to come and teach his children self-defense. He wanted them to be able to defend themselves if someone tried to take them or to hurt them. He had a big gym built for them, and he and their mom also took the classes with their children.

"The children loved the classes and begged for more when the classes ended. So, the judge looked around for something else the children could do. He thought karate looked like fun, and the children agreed. They soon mastered the beginner classes and moved up to earn more belts. They had their dad look around for something else for them to learn. He discovered kickboxing. He asked the children if they wanted to try it. The two older children had become interested in other things, but the two younger girls were excited about learning something new. They enjoyed the classes and often sparred with each other when class was over.

"The judge also thought the children should learn to handle weapons. He had them taken to the police firing range and let the policemen teach them the proper way to handle and fire weapons. The two younger sisters excelled at the firing range and soon entered local competitions. One of the sisters beat out all the other people taking part and became the local champion. The girls were growing bored with shooting practice, so they returned to their other interests. They focused on kickboxing."

Ruby had been standing in the door listening and

she came forward. "I think it is time for you girls to go to bed. It has been a long day," she said to the girls.

"But Mom, we want to hear the story," said one of the girls.

"Maybe Miss Dora will finish the story tomorrow," she said.

"Sure, I will," said Dora. "Good night, girls. I will see you in the morning."

Ruby ushered the girls out the door and into the next room. When she went through the partially open door, Dora saw Rafe and Blake working on putting in the safety gate. They had been listening to her story, as well. Dora smiled at Rafe, and he smiled back at her.

"What Dora did not say," Blake said quietly, "was she got her black belt in karate by the age of ten. She was the district sharpshooting champion. And she was the state kickboxing champion for three years, starting at the age of fourteen."

"Why did she stop?" asked Rafe.

"She said she wanted to give someone else a chance. She was ready to go to college. She has always wanted to be a teacher. She has a way with children. You saw the way she had those in there hanging on her every word." Blake smiled. "She's quite a lady, my sister," he said proudly.

"Yes, she is," agreed Rafe. They finished the gate and went to get the cot to be set up in the closet.

Dora handed the baby over to his mother. She folded a blanket to put in the cradle. After seeing the baby settle in, she went downstairs and got a large garbage bag. She took it upstairs and, with Ruby's help, removed all of Sylvia's clothes and stuffed them into the bag. She dragged the bag into the hall.

Rafe and Blake came in carrying the cot and its mattress. Dora went and got a pillow, some small sheets, and a blanket. Lester watched them make the bed and was grinning. "This is great," he said. "I never had my own room before."

Ruby gave him a hug and shooed him off to bed. "Thank you all for all of your help," she said.

Dora came over and gave her a hug. "I will send Harry up when he gets back with the formula. Let me know if you need anything." Dora hugged her again, and she, Rafe, and Blake said goodnight and went downstairs. They collected the laundry and garbage bag on the way. Rafe took the bedding into the laundry room, and Blake left the garbage bag by the back door.

CHAPTER 7

*D*ora, Rafe, and Blake got drinks out of the refrigerator and started to the living room to relax. The door to the kitchen apartment opened, and Mrs. Amory entered the room.

"Oh, Mrs. Amory, I hope we did not disturb you," said Dora.

"No, dear, I just wanted to get some water to take my medicine with. I will be retiring then."

"Would you like something to eat?" asked Dora.

"No, I am not hungry. I just need the water," she said.

Dora took down a glass and filled it with water for her. "If you get hungry, just help yourself from the refrigerator," said Dora. She motioned to the two men. "This is my brother, Blake, and this is Rafe Haggerty."

"Blake and I introduced ourselves earlier, and I know Rafe from school," Mrs. Amory replied. They all smiled and said goodnight. Mrs. Amory returned to her room with her glass of water.

They started out again, but Maddie entered, followed closely by Jason and Harry. "I have the formula. I bought it in cans already mixed, so all we have to do is pour it into bottles and heat it up for the baby. I got some extra bottles and a couple of large packages of diapers. I also bought some other baby supplies." Maddie paused to take a breath.

"You did great," said Dora approvingly. "Let's wash these bottles and get some formula ready for the baby. You guys can go on into the front and relax for a while," Dora told the men with a smile. Dora and Maddie got busy washing bottles and sterilizing them for the formula.

The guys hurriedly left before Dora found something else for them to do. The guys settled onto the sofa and chairs. "Is there always so much going on with your sisters?" Jason asked Blake.

Blake smiled. "Most of the time, Maddie is just getting started, but she looks up to Dora, and she is quick to follow where Dora leads. She could not have a better role model. I am very proud of my sisters. Dora has a thing about families staying together if the children are safe. Children come first with her. When she was fifteen, on top of a full load at school and her kickboxing championship, she did volunteer work at the local women's shelter in Rolling Fork. She loved working there." He paused. "There was one woman who stayed there. She had two little girls. She claimed to be afraid of her husband. Dora noticed how the girls seemed to be afraid of their mother. They would cringe whenever she said anything to them. Well, Dora started to check out the woman's story. She talked to the woman's mother.

"The mother told her it was all nonsense. She said the girls' dad was the gentlest person alive. She said her daughter was depressed and having spells of paranoia. She said the father was worried sick about his girls. So, Dora went around and talked to their friends and neighbors. They all told the same story. Dora went back and talked to the woman. She told her what she found out. The woman broke down and cried. She called her husband to come and pick them up. Dora said those girls were so happy to see their dad. They ran to him and didn't want to let go of him.

"Dora still was not satisfied. She was worried the woman would revert to her former behavior if she did not get help. So, Dora went to the Judge and persuaded him to have the woman talk to a doctor and get help. The woman is still in treatment and doing well. Dora checks on her regularly."

The men were all quiet when Blake finished telling about Dora. He had given them a lot to think about. Rafe smiled to himself. He was satisfied with all he learned about Dora. He only hoped she would be as satisfied with him and his family.

Blake looked over at Rafe and grinned. He talked about Dora for Rafe's benefit. His mom had told him about the mirror. He was all for true love, but he wanted them to go into any relationship with their eyes open and knowing what to expect. Rafe looked like a nice guy, and he was certainly attracted to Dora. He had barely kept his eyes off Dora the entire time since they'd arrived at the house. Blake would give them a thumbs-up for love.

Maddie and Dora fixed four bottles of formula and heated one. They put the others in the refrigerator for later. They took the heated bottle, the diapers, and the bag of baby supplies up to Ruby. They piled everything on a bench, and Dora took the bottle over to Ruby so she could feed the baby.

"Just take it slow," said Dora. "He cannot take a lot at a time. Let him drink a bit then burp him, and when he starts moving around, feed him some more. Babies get more air from bottle feeding than breastfeeding, so you must burp them more frequently. We have three more bottles made downstairs in the refrigerator. If you need them during the night, just heat them to warm them slightly, so the milk is warm like your breast milk. If you feed them to him cold, it will make his tummy hurt." They all three laughed at Dora's remarks. She continued, unfazed. "Maddie and I will go and send Harry up so you guys can get some rest. We will see you in the morning. Goodnight," said Dora. Maddie just smiled as they left.

Dora peeped into the girl's room as they left. They were all sleeping soundly. When they arrived back downstairs, they found Harry about to fall asleep. "Harry," said Dora. "Why don't you join Ruby and get some sleep?"

Harry got out of his chair and wished everyone a good night. He headed for the stairs. He was looking forward to the best night's sleep he had enjoyed in a while.

Dora went over and sat next to Rafe. He put his arm around her and pulled her closer to his side. They smiled at each other, and Dora laid her head on his chest.

"Tired?" Rafe whispered.

"A little," said Dora. "It has been a very eventful day. Not what I was expecting at all."

Rafe laughed softly. "I'll bet."

"I'm glad I did not have to wait to meet you. It

saves me a lot of time," she said. "Now, we can begin getting to know each other."

"Oh, I think we have a head start on getting to know each other, and I like everything I know," said Rafe.

"Wait a minute," said Jason, who had been listening to their conversation. "I thought you two already knew each other."

Maddie and Blake were grinning broadly at them. Dora glanced up at Rafe and then looked over at Jason. "Rafe and I met in a magic mirror," she said.

"A magic mirror," said Jason. "There is no such thing."

"Yes, there is," said Dora. "It only works for girls. It sometimes shows them their one true love."

"If it only works for girls, how did Rafe know about you?" asked Jason.

"He was standing in front of a reflective surface, and the magic mirror allowed for us to have brief conversations. We had no control over what it was going to show or when," explained Dora

"Where is this mirror? Can I see it?" asked Jason.

"It is in a display in an art gallery in Rolling Fork," replied Dora.

"How did you know who Rafe was and where he lived?" asked Jason.

"He told me his name, and my mom told me where he lived. She is friends with your mother. Maddie is named after your mother. Our mothers have been corresponding for years, ever since my family moved away from here."

Jason looked at Rafe. Rafe grinned at him. "It's all true," he said.

"Well, I'll be," declared Jason, sitting back and

laughing. Blake and Maddie laughed also. Rafe and Dora just snuggled closer to each other.

There was a knock on the door. Blake went to answer it. He opened it to find a bunch of people. They looked remarkably like Rafe and Jason. "You must be the Haggerty family." Blake smiled. "Come in."

He stood back and let them enter. There were two teen girls, one teen boy, their mother, carrying a small girl, and a small boy following the group.

"Uncle Rafe," called the small girl, squirming to get down. As soon as she got down, she flung herself onto Rafe and Dora. Rafe caught her up and gave her a hug.

Dora moved over and got up to greet Rafe's mother. "Hello, Mrs. Haggerty. It's nice to meet you," said Dora, going over and offering her hand. Madeline ignored the hand and pulled her into a hug. Dora hugged her back.

"I would not have intruded tonight, but your mother and the Judge called me when they could not get a hold of you on your phone. They said neither you nor Maddie were answering. They wanted to know if everything was all right."

Dora took her phone out and checked it. "It needs charging," she said.

Maddie took her phone out and looked at it. "I must have accidently turned it off," she said.

'Do you know the number for Mom and Dad on Ship to Shore?" asked Dora. She looked at Madeline enquiringly.

"Yes, Lucy gave it to me. She said the Judge was threatening to get a helicopter and fly back."

"Oh, my goodness," said Dora as she dialed the number Madeline gave her.

"Hello, Maddie," said Lucy.

"No, Mom, this is Dora. My phone needs charging. Maddie had her phone off. There is no need for you to worry. We are fine. I called Blake and asked him to join us. He is here also."

"Hello, Dora, what is going on? Why is Blake there?" asked the Judge.

"We are fine, Dad. Don't worry," said Dora.

"Every time you say don't worry, I know there is something to worry about," said the Judge.

Dora sighed. She never could fool the Judge. "We had a few little problems, but we worked them all out. Well, almost all. I called Blake to take care of one more thing tomorrow. By the way, Cousin Sylvia has been dead for three years. We found out when we got here," said Dora.

"Why wasn't I told?" asked the Judge.

"Blake is going to ask Mills and Mills about it tomorrow."

"Are you sure you don't need me to fly back?"

"I'm sure, Dad. You and Mom enjoy your cruise. If we can't handle things, we will call you at once to come back. Blake and Maddie send their love. I love you both. Tell Mom to enjoy the trip. You rest up and enjoy yourself. Good night."

Dora hung up the phone with a sigh of relief. "I think he will stay put for now," she said.

Rafe was grinning broadly, and Blake and Maddie burst out laughing.

"You sure managed some fancy footwork," said Jason admiringly.

Dora just shrugged and turned and grinned at

Rafe. "Please, have a seat and join us," she said to Madeline.

"Blake, would you bring in a couple of chairs from the dining room?" Dora asked.

Jason went with Blake to help bring in more chairs. When everyone had chairs, Dora went back over to where Rafe was seated, cuddling Dede, and picking up Lars, she sat down beside Rafe and cuddled Lars in her lap.

She leaned against Rafe and smiled at Dede. "Hi, Dede. You sure are a cutie," she whispered. Dede reached over a hand and rubbed Dora's face.

"You're pretty," Dede declared.

"Thank you," said Dora, smiling.

She pulled Lars closer and gave him a hug. Lars smiled up at her. He was perfectly content sitting in her lap. Rafe smiled at her. He was so happy the children liked her.

The rest of the group had been talking quietly while watching Rafe and Dora. "Lucy told me about you seeing Rafe in a magic mirror," said Madeline.

"Wait a minute!" exclaimed Jason. "You knew about the magic mirror."

"Of course," said Madeline. "Lucy told me about it years ago. She and the Judge met through one in Italy."

"It was the same mirror," said Dora. "The owner of the gallery bought it and two others in a recent trip to Italy. Mom and Dad had tried to buy it when they met, but the man in the antique store would not sell it to them. He said he bought them for his three daughters. When the owners of the gallery were over there, the old man said his daughters had found their true loves and were all happily married. He said he no longer needed them. He said it was time for the mirrors to help others. It has created quite a stir in Rolling Fork."

"Are all of the mirrors in Rolling Fork?" asked Meg, the older teen girl.

"No, they have one display in the art gallery in Rolling Fork. They fixed up one of the mirrors for their daughter, Valerie, to display in the museum in Denton. The last mirror is being displayed in a small town in Kansas."

"Mom, we are going to have to make a trip to see one of those mirrors," Meg told her mom with a grin.

"Maybe in a couple of years, when you are older," her mom replied. "It was good to see you, Dora, Maddie, and Blake. Come over anytime and visit. After all, we are almost family. Right now, I need to get these two home and in bed. I'm glad it all worked out with your folks. If you need help with anything, just call. I'll send Rafe right over," Madeline finished up, laughing.

She started to come and take Dede, but Dede tightened her little arms around Rafe and refused to let go. Rafe got up, carrying her out of the house. Dora carried Lars out to the van. Rafe put Dede into her seat. Then, he turned and took Lars from Dora to put him in his seat. He gave both children a kiss and told them he would be home soon. Dora and Rafe stood outside as everyone else piled into the van and left for home.

Rafe put his arm around Dora and kissed her gently. "I need to go and let you get some rest." He hugged her close. "I sure hate to leave you," he whispered.

"Me, too," said Dora. "But I will still be here tomorrow."

He kissed her one more time, and they went inside to collect Jason. "Come on, Jason. We need to go and let Dora, Maddie, and Blake get some rest," said Rafe when they went inside.

Jason stood up and turned to Dora. "Will you kick me if I give you a hug?" he asked.

"Not this time," she assured him with a smile.

Jason gave her a hug. When he let her go, he looked at her and grinned. "I'm glad you are going to be around. With you around, I know life will never be boring." He laughed, and everyone else laughed with him.

"Do you think the grocery store will still be open?" he asked Rafe. "We never picked up our order."

"It should be. I think it stays open late tonight. We can drive by and see," replied Rafe.

Rafe leaned over and kissed Dora one more time, and then they were gone.

CHAPTER 8

ora looked at Maddie, who was bursting with excitement. Then she remembered about Liam. With so much going on, she had forgotten about Maddie seeing Liam in the mirror.

Dora shushed her when she started to say something about it. Dora nodded toward Blake. She did not want to have to ask him to keep quiet about Maddie seeing Liam in the mirror.

Blake looked at the girls suspiciously, but then he said goodnight. He gave each girl a hug and reminded them to lock all the doors. Then he changed his mind and went to check on the doors himself. When he left out the front door, he waited to hear the lock click before going to his apartment.

Maddie started talking as soon as she was sure Blake was gone. "He smiled at me and I smiled back, and he kept glancing at me and looking away quickly when he saw me noticing. He is so handsome," she declared.

"Just remember, you both have some growing up to do," said Dora. She reached over and gave Maddie a hug. "It will be the start of a great adventure," she declared. "True love is always a great adventure when you answer the call."

Dora and Maddie went upstairs. They were careful to close and lock the gate at the top of the stairs. They did not want any children falling down the stairs in the middle of the night.

They had been so busy getting everyone else settled that they had neglected to fix their own beds. Since they brought their own bedding from home, it only took a few minutes to strip and remake the beds. Each of their rooms had bathrooms attached, so they each had a quick shower and crawled into bed.

Dora stretched out and thought about Rafe. She smiled. He was everything she could wish for. His children were adorable. They were going to make a wonderful family. Dora's eyes drifted closed, and she was soon soundly asleep. Maddie was also sleeping with a happy smile on her face.

The next morning, Blake let himself into the house with a key he had gotten from Dora. When he entered, he heard a phone ringing. He realized it was Dora's, still sitting on the charger from the night before. He went to answer it before it could wake everyone up. "Hello," he said.

"Who is this?" asked a male voice.

"This is Blake Hawthorn. Who is this?" he asked.

"This is Police Chief Stan Welldon. I thought I was calling Miss Dora's phone."

"You did. Her phone was downstairs on the

charger. Dora is still sleeping. Can I help you?" asked Blake.

"I told Miss Dora I would keep her updated about Miss Deeton. She has called in an attorney, Derrick Mills, to try to get her out on bail. He is down at the cell with her now. They are having a shouting match. He has called her some very unflattering names. She returned the favor."

"I'll be right down. Stall them. Do not let him get her out. There is a good chance we will be filing charges against him, also," said Blake. "Oh, Chief, where do I find the jail?"

"It is one block down Main Street from the bank. It is on the right if you are coming from Hawthorn house."

"Thanks, I will be right there."

Blake walked into the jail about ten minutes later. He walked up to the desk and asked for Chief Welldon. The chief, hearing his name, came over to the desk to greet him. He stuck out his hand for a handshake and grinned.

"Blake Hawthorn, I presume," he said. "The Hawthorn family is making quite a stir in this town."

"Yes," agreed Blake with a smile. "We tend to do that, especially if Dora is around."

"Are Miss Deeton and Derrick Mills still around?" he asked.

"Yes, come with me. I'll take you down so you can enjoy the show they are putting on." Blake followed the chief as he led the way to where Sylvia and Derrick were loudly discussing her arrest.

"If you were not such a greedy bitch, you would not be here. Why did you have to try and sell the furnishings in the house?" shouted a voice.

"I needed the money. You kept doling it out in such small amounts, I did not have enough," answered Sylvia.

"You are just spoiled. I could live a year on what you were spending a month," he answered.

"Are you going to help me get out of here?" she asked.

He paused for a minute.

"I suppose I will have to see what I can do," he answered.

Blake and the chief had been standing and listening. They had not been noticed by the other two. They were too busy arguing.

"I do not think so," said Blake. Both turned to stare at Blake.

"Who are you?" demanded Derrick Mills.

"I'm your worst nightmare," replied Blake with a smile.

"Don't you think it is a conflict of interest for you to represent Miss Deeton when you are representing Judge Hawthorn and the Judge is charging her with stealing from him?" asked Blake.

Derrick turned pale. "How did you know about Judge Hawthorn?" he asked.

"Because I have his power of attorney, and you are under suspicion of being Miss Deeton's accomplice. You will have all of Judge Hawthorn's records for the last three years ready for inspection. An investigator from the Attorney General's office will be contacting you later today. In the meantime, all your financial accounts have been frozen until further notice. So, Miss Deeton will have to look for another attorney. And Miss Deeton, all your accounts have been frozen until it is determined how much money you have stolen from the Judge. Have a good day."

Blake and the chief turned and left. The chief was grinning widely. He held out his hand to Blake. "It is great to have your family in town. How did you get things done so quickly?"

"I called the Attorney General last night before I went to bed. I interned in his office for two years. He was glad to help," Blake replied.

The chief laughed. "Give Miss Dora and Miss Maddie my regards, and I'll let you know if anything happens."

"Thanks, Chief Welldon," said Blake.

Blake headed for his car to go back to the house. While he was unlocking it, he heard Derrick Mills storm out of the station, slam into his car, and speed off with smoking wheels. Blake grinned. "He was in a hurry," he murmured.

When Blake returned home, Dora and Maddie were in the kitchen with three young girls. They were all happily chatting while Dora and Maddie made pancakes. Blake came over to the stove and looked at the cooking pancakes. "They look good. Do you have enough for me?" he asked.

"I think we can manage one or two for you," said Maddie.

"Your car was gone when we got up," stated Dora.

"Yes," agreed Blake. "The chief called to keep you updated, and I went down to the station to meet him. He sends his regards to you and Maddie."

"Was there a problem?" asked Dora.

"No, I just told Derrick Mills he could not represent Miss Deeton because it would be a conflict of interest since the Judge is already his client," said Blake. "I also told both of them their accounts have been frozen, and the Attorney General's office is sending an investigator to look into the accounts he has been handling for the Judge the last three years."

"Wow," said Dora. "When did you get all of this done?"

"I called the Attorney General last night. He got everything into motion," grinned Blake.

"Great," said Dora with a big smile. "Sit down and eat." She put a plate in front of him. It was stacked high with pancakes. She pushed the syrup and butter closer to him and stood back.

"I can't eat all of this," exclaimed Blake, but he picked up his fork and dug in.

Dora piled pancakes on the plates as Maddie held them, then Maddie passed them around to the girls. Maddie put two more plates on the table for Dora and herself. They joined everyone at the table to eat. Dora looked around at the girls. They were enjoying their pancakes, but they watched Blake wide-eyed as he made inroads in his large stack of pancakes. Dora and Maddie grinned. They were used to Blake's appetite.

"Hi, girls, are your brothers and parents still sleeping?" asked Blake.

The girls nodded their heads shyly.

"They have had a rough time of it lately," said Dora. "When we found the girls were awake, we brought them down to eat. I thought their parents could use a sleep in." She had just finished speaking when Lester came into the dining room.

"Good morning, Lester," said Maddie. "Have a seat. I'll bring you some pancakes."

Lester hurriedly climbed into a chair, and Maddie rose to bring him a plate of pancakes. She also poured him a glass of orange juice. She refilled the girls' glasses. When she started to set the juice down, Blake held up his glass to be filled. Maddie smilingly filled his glass and sat down at the table.

"Are your parents still sleeping, Lester?" asked Dora.

"Yes," he nodded. "I slipped by real quiet so I wouldn't wake them."

"Good." Dora smiled.

Everyone was quiet as they ate their pancakes. When they were finished, Maddie took the children to wash their hands and faces. Blake helped Dora to clear the table and put the dishes into the dishwasher.

"What did you think of Derrick Mills?" asked Dora.

"I think he is a first-class jerk," replied Blake. "There is not a doubt in my mind about him being in on everything with Sylvia Deeton, everything except selling the furnishings. He probably would have gone along with her on selling the furnishings, too, if she had offered him a portion of the money. They are both too greedy to share. I hope the Attorney General's office can make a case against him."

"Me, too," agreed Dora. "I really do not want to have to teach him what happens when you mess with the Hawthorns." She paused for a moment. "It might be fun to watch him sweat," she said.

Blake grinned at her. He fully agreed with her sentiments about Derrick Mills. "What do you have planned for today?" he asked.

"I am going to have a discussion with a certain head of Child Protective Services. I intend to find out for sure who called in a complaint against Harry's family. When I find out, I am going to talk to the informant in person. I have an idea who it was, but I want to be sure," declared Dora grimly.

"If you need any help, or a lawyer to keep you out of jail, let me know," said Blake with a grin.

CHAPTER 9

When Dora was getting ready to leave, Rafe knocked on the front door. Dora opened the door and smiled up at him. "Good morning," she said, smiling.

Rafe leaned forward and kissed her gently. "Good morning. Are you headed somewhere?" he asked.

"Yes, I am going to pay that social worker's boss a visit. I want to know the name of the person trying to cause trouble for Harry and his family."

"Would you like me to take you? I know where the office is located. It will save you having to look for it. Besides, I just want to be with you," Rafe admitted.

"Okay, it will be nice to have company, and I want to be with you, too," Dora said.

"We can go in my truck," said Rafe. "We can leave the car for Maddie to use if she needs it."

"Maddie is looking after the children while their parents are still sleeping," said Dora.

"Jason is going to come by and take Harry to file his workman's comp claim later this morning," said Rafe. "He did not want to bother you too early. I think he is a little afraid of you."

"Why is he afraid of me? I would never harm Jason." Dora looked puzzled.

Rafe laughed. "I do not think Jason has ever met a woman like you. He is used to girls trying to play up to him. They all act dependent on him. He hardly knows how to act around someone who can stand up for herself and does not expect to be rescued."

"Well, he will have to get used to me because I'm not going away," said Dora firmly. Rafe grinned and squeezed her hand.

Rafe parked in front of the Child Protective Services building. He and Dora got out, and he held her hand as he escorted her inside. Once inside, Dora looked around and headed for the greeter's desk.

"Good morning," said Dora. "Is the manager here?"

"Yes, do you have an appointment?"

Dora smiled at her sweetly. "No, I just wanted to check and be sure my friend called in about those children in the bad part of town," Dora said quietly.

The girl looked at her computer screen, and then she scrolled back a way. "Oh, yes, Mrs. Matthews called it in yesterday. It has been taken care of," said the girl.

Dora smiled at her. "Thank you."

"Who are you, and what do you want?" asked a snarly voice from a nearby door.

Dora turned and looked at the woman hard. "My name is Dora Hawthorn, and this is Rafe Haggerty," she told the woman. "Who are you?"

"I'm Nora Smart. I'm in charge here. And I know Mr. Haggerty," she replied. "What do you want?"

Dora glanced at Rafe. "She tried to stop me from adopting Dede and Lars," he told Dora quietly.

Dora looked back at the woman. "I want to talk to you. Do you want to have this discussion here, or do we go to your office?" Dora asked.

The woman stared at her hard for a moment then motioned for them to follow her to her office. "What is this about?" she asked.

"I understand it is policy to snatch children from their parents and break up families instead of trying to help keep families together," said Dora.

"We do not have the time or resources to try to help families. It is our job to take children out of bad situations and put them where they are safe," Nora informed them.

"You do not take the family into consideration at all?" Dora inquired.

"That is not my job," stated Nora.

"Well, it is about to be part of your job. There are going to be some changes around here. You can be part of those changes, or you can look for another job," said Dora.

"You can't fire me or tell me how to run my office," said Nora.

"Maybe I can't, but the governor and the attorney general can. There is a representative from the attorney general's office in town now. As soon as he takes care of the business he is attending to, I will have him check in here. The governor most certainly can fire you. So, Miss Smart, I would suggest you start changing your policies and start trying to help families instead of tearing them apart." Dora finished this speech and turned to leave.

Rafe hurried to open the door for her. He couldn't stop grinning. When they got outside, Rafe took Dora into his arms and hugged her. "Where to now?" he asked.

"Do you know where Mrs. Matthews lives?" asked Dora.

"Yes, everybody knows where that busybody lives," said Rafe, holding the door so Dora could get into the truck.

"Well," said Dora. "Let's go have a little talk with the local busybody."

Rafe smiled widely as he got into the truck. He had not had this much fun in years.

When they were in the truck and on their way, Dora turned to Rafe. "You said she tried to stop you from adopting Dede and Lars. How was it any of her business?" she asked.

"She made it her business. She went before the court and argued for them to be placed in a two-parent home. She said since I was not married, I could not give them the care and stability they needed. Lucky for me, the judge hearing the case was an old family friend. He knew there was no better place for them. He told her to stay out of it and get back to cases in need of her attention. I was lucky he knew us and did not pay any attention to her."

"I was going to give her the benefit of the doubt, but I am going to have to keep an eye on her. I also need to check into her former placements. I do not trust her. I need to see if I can find a replacement for her. Her attitude is all wrong for the office she oversees," Dora finished with a sigh.

Rafe squeezed her hand as he stopped in front of a house in an affluent neighborhood. Before they exited the truck, Rafe turned to Dora. "I'm pretty sure Mrs. Matthews is the one who called and got CPS on the case about Dede and Lars. I can't prove it, but I am sure she did it," he said.

Dora's mouth firmed. "Let's go talk to Mrs. Matthews."

After knocking, Dora waited for the door to be answered. Dora could feel someone peering through the peep hole in the door. She knocked firmly again. She wanted her to know she was not going away.

The door opened slowly. The woman, who she remembered from the bank, looked back at her. "What do you want?" asked Mrs. Matthews rudely.

Dora smiled. "Why, I just want to come in and meet my neighbor," she said sweetly. Mrs. Matthews looked at her suspiciously but reluctantly moved back and allowed them to enter. "Hello, Mrs. Matthews. I'm Dora Hawthorn, and you know Rafe Haggerty."

"Yes, I know Mr. Haggerty, and I know who you are. You are the one who kept that bank robber out of jail."

"I wanted to talk to you about your call to Child Protective Services. You tried to get Harry's children taken away from him and his wife," said Dora.

"I don't know what you are talking about," said Mrs. Matthews. "Anyway, a bank robber should not be raising children."

"Well, lucky for everyone, you are not the one to decide about who should or should not raise children," said Dora. "Harry and his family are now part of my family. As is Mr. Haggerty and his family. If I hear any gossip spread about any of my family, I will be very upset."

"It's a free country. We have the right to express our opinion," stated Mrs. Matthews smugly.

"Exactly," agreed Dora, with a smile. "Now, if

someone spread a rumor about your family money being obtained through drug money, even if you are cleared, a lot of people will still believe it is true and that you paid your way out of trouble, especially if you are audited by the IRS right after the rumor goes its rounds. Do I make myself clear?"

Mrs. Matthews turned very pale. She looked at Dora and glanced at Rafe. "I understand perfectly, Miss Hawthorn. No one will hear a word from me."

"Good day, Mrs. Matthews," said Dora.

She and Rafe turned to leave. Rafe nodded to Mrs. Matthews, but he did not say anything. He was in a hurry to get out of there before he started laughing. Rafe was still chuckling to himself when he pulled to a stop in front of Hawthorn house. He reached over and hugged Dora to him. She smiled back at him.

"You just have to talk to people in a language they understand," she said. "I learned that from the Judge."

Rafe laughed again. "I love you. I love your whole family. I am so glad you looked into the magic mirror."

"Me, too," agreed Dora.

She leaned forward for Rafe's kiss. The kiss was interrupted by a knocking on the driver's window.

CHAPTER 10

"**B**reak it up in there," demanded Jason.

Rafe sighed and leaned his forehead against Dora's. "Jason, don't you have something else to do?" he asked.

"Yeah, as soon as Dora tells Harry he can go with me, I will take him and get his workman's comp started and see what job he can do," said Jason impatiently.

Dora laughed and turned to get out of the truck. Rafe pulled her back for one more quick kiss. He told her to stay right there. He got out and went around the truck to open her door and help her out.

They followed Jason inside, where they found Harry and Ruby sitting in the front room. Ruby was feeding the baby a bottle, while Harry looked on proudly.

"Where's the girls and Lester?" asked Dora.

"Mrs. Amory and Maddie took them all to Mrs. Amory's room to watch cartoons on TV," said Ruby. "I think she misses being around children since she retired."

"Good," said Dora. She turned to Harry. "Harry,

you can go with Jason and let him fix you up with insurance and a job. Jason, make sure no one causes Harry any trouble."

Jason saluted. "Yes, Ma'am," he said smartly. Harry and Jason left after Harry leaned over and kissed the baby and Ruby.

"Did you and Harry get something to eat?" asked Dora.

"Yes, Maddie made us some pancakes," answered Ruby.

"Good," said Dora with a smile. "If you get hungry, help yourself to whatever is in the refrigerator."

"Thanks," answered Ruby. She looked at Dora curiously. "Why are you being so nice to us?"

"You are my family now. I always try to see my family has everything they need." Dora smiled at Ruby gently.

Dora turned to Rafe, who had been sitting quietly, listening to Dora and Ruby talk. She smiled at him and reached over and took his hand. Rafe smiled back and squeezed her hand.

The front door opened, and Blake entered accompanied by a gentleman. "Hi, everyone," said Blake.

Everyone answered, "Hi," back to him.

"This is Mr. Markum. He is the representative from the attorney general's office. Mr. Markum, this is my sister Dora, Rafe Haggerty, and a friend of ours, Ruby Wells." He motioned toward each one as he said their names. Rafe and Dora rose and shook hands with Mr. Markum. Ruby just nodded to him.

"Have a seat, Mr. Markum. How is it going with Mills and Mills?" asked Dora.

"We are not finished yet. There is definitely enough evidence already to bring charges against Derrick Mills. I have forwarded information to the Board of Attorneys. I imagine he will be disbarred."

"While you are here, I wonder if you could check on something else," said Dora.

"What is it you are worried about?" asked Mr. Markum.

"It is about the head of Child Protective Services. Nora Smart oversees CPS and is very ridged in her practices. She does not try to help the families stay together. She just snatches the children away from their parents and puts them in foster care. I would like to see all the cases she has overseen and have the children checked on. We need to know what kind of situations she is putting the children into and if they can be returned to their parents." Dora paused for a breath.

"We do not have an investigator qualified to handle looking into CPS," said Mr. Markum.

"There is a lady in Rolling Fork. She has just gotten her doctorate in child services. She has been volunteering at the ladies' shelter to do her internship. She is a trained professional, but she still has compassion for the people who need help. She would be the perfect one for the job. Maybe later she could be offered Mrs. Smart's job. Mrs. Smart needs to be where she does not have so much authority over children's lives. The person in Rolling Fork's name is Sara Glen." Dora stopped and waited for Mr. Markum's answer.

Mr. Markum had been taking notes all the while Dora was talking. "I'll bring this matter to the attorney general's immediate attention," he said.

"Thank you, Mr. Markum," said Dora.

"Thank you. I wish everyone was as willing to go the extra step to help. You are an inspiration," he said, smiling. Rafe, Blake, and even Ruby were smiling with satisfaction.

"Would you like something to drink, Mr. Markum?" asked Dora.

"I would like a cola, if you have it," he replied.

"Blake, could you bring Mr. Markum a drink?" asked Dora.

Blake got up and went to get a cola for Mr. Markum. "Would anyone else like a drink while I'm in the kitchen?" he asked.

"Yes, please, thank you," answered Dora and Rafe.

He looked at Ruby. She shook her head. "I'll be right back."

Dora and Rafe were sitting on the sofa next to each other. Ruby finished feeding the baby his bottle and put a cloth over her shoulder so she could burp him. There was an immediate loud burp. Everyone laughed.

"What a loud sound from such a small person," said Mr. Markum, smiling.

Blake returned with the drinks and passed them out. Ruby excused herself to go and put the baby down for a nap. They drank their colas and chatted quietly for a while.

"The attorney general asked me to tell you he would love to have you in his office this summer, if you can make time for us," Mr. Markum said to Blake.

Blake smiled. "I don't think I can make it this summer. My parents are taking a much-anticipated cruise. They expect me to hang around here and watch out for my sisters."

"I understand. I'll pass your regrets on, and if you talk to your parents, tell them we all wish them a great vacation." Mr. Markum got out of his seat and prepared to leave. "I had better go. I must get in touch with the attorney general and get a warrant started for Derrick Mills. I will also tell him about your concerns with Child Protective Services, Miss Dora."

"Thank you, Mr. Markum," said Dora.

They all got up and walked him to the door. After he left, they returned to their seats. Dora looked thoughtful. Rafe looked at her curiously. "What's wrong?" he asked.

"I was just thinking about Derrick's father. He and Dad were friends. He took care of everything the way the Judge wanted until his health forced him to retire. I would hate for him to learn about what Derrick has been up to, and his arrest, through some local gossip," she said.

"Do you think we should go and see him?" asked Blake.

"I think it is what Dad would expect us to do," she said.

"All right," said Blake. "I'll go and tell Maddie where we are going."

Blake headed for the back of the house to talk to Maddie, and Dora turned to Rafe. "Do you want me to go with you?" he asked.

"I was hoping you would," answered Dora.

Blake returned with Maddie. "The children are not going to be too much for Mrs. Amory, are they?" she asked Maddie.

"I'm keeping an eye on them all. I'll feed them a

snack in a little while. I think Mrs. Amory has missed being around children. She is sitting back, watching them enjoy television, and smiling. We will be fine. I will see you all in a little while. Why don't you pick up some pizzas on the way home?" asked Maddie.

"What a great idea," said Dora, smiling. "I could enjoy some pizza tonight."

Maddie waved them off, and they decided to go in Blake's car instead of Rafe's truck. Rafe sat in front with Blake, so he could tell him where to go. Dora took the back seat.

Rafe guided them to a house in a good neighborhood. It was a nice house, but it needed some yard work done. It looked like Derrick had not been taking very good care of it since his father had been ill.

They all three got out of the car. Rafe managed to get Dora's door open and help her out before she could open the door herself. She smiled up at him sweetly. They all went to the front door, and Blake knocked loudly.

"If he is old and ill, he may be hard of hearing," said Blake.

They all heard the tap of a cane coming toward the front door. The door opened slowly, and Mr. Mills looked at them enquiringly.

"May I help you?" he asked.

Dora stepped forward. "Mr. Mills, I'm Dora Hawthorn. This is my brother, Blake, and our friend Rafe Haggerty. May we come in?"

Mr. Mills smiled and stepped back to allow them entrance. "How is the Judge doing these days?" he asked.

"He is doing fine," said Blake. "He is taking Mom

on a cruise. We knew he would want us to stop and check on you while we are here."

"I'm glad you stopped by. I don't get many visitors these days," he replied.

They all took seats, and Mr. Mills looked at them enquiringly.

"Mr. Mills, did you know about our cousin Sylvia dying three years ago?" asked Dora.

Mr. Mills looked startled. "No, Derrick has not mentioned it."

"He did not mention it because he did not let the Judge know. Sylvia had a nurse. Her name was Sylvia also. She continued to live in Hawthorn house and collect the allowance and enjoy the other accounts the Judge had set up. Derrick continued to pay for all the household expenses out of the Judge's funds. When I arrived here yesterday, I was just in time to stop the sale of a large load of antiques from Hawthorn house. We came over here to tell you all of this because we did not want you to be blindsided by it. Sylvia Deeton is already in jail. Derrick's accounts have been frozen until he has been audited. He will most likely be arrested also."

Mr. Mills looked like he was about ready to cry. He just shook his head. "This is my fault," he said.

"This is not your fault," said Dora.

"I knew Derrick had problems. I should have kept a better eye on him," he said.

"Derrick is a grown man, and you have been sick. There is no reason for you to take his misdeeds on your shoulders. I know the Judge would feel the same way. When he gets home from his cruise he will probably come here and tell you the same thing. I'm sorry we had to bring you such sad news," said Dora.

"No, don't be sorry. I appreciate you coming to tell me in person. A lot of people would have just left me to find out through gossip. I can tell your mom and dad did well with you kids," he said.

They all rose and followed Mr. Mills to the door. He stood watching them from the doorway. Dora waved as they pulled away. Mr. Mills waved back.

CHAPTER 11

They stopped at the pizza place on the way home and bought enough pizza, bread sticks, cinnamon sticks, cheese sticks, chicken wings, and pasta to feed a small army.

When they had it, all loaded in the car and were on their way again, Dora told Rafe to call his mother and tell her to bring the children over for pizza. After getting her agreement, they made a quick stop and picked up paper plates and cups. Dora said there was no way was she going to try finding enough real plates for the crowd.

They unloaded the pizza at home. Jason and Harry were there, and they helped to bring everything into the dining room. The kids must have smelled the pizza because they came crowding into the dining room with big smiles on their faces. They were ready for a treat.

Blake and Jason found a small children's table in the pantry. They put it in the corner of the dining room. Dora and Maggie sat the children at the table and started passing out paper plates filled with food. Mrs. Amory joined them at the big table.

She was looking a lot better than she had the day before.

There was a loud knock at the door, and Dora went to answer it. She gave Rafe's mother a big smile and invited the group in. Meg was carrying Dede, and Liam had Lars. "Come on in, pizza is in the dining room. Help yourself," said Dora.

Dede spotted Rafe and squirmed to get down. Lars reached for Dora as soon as he was close to her. She reached over and took him from Liam and gave him a hug. She smiled at Liam.

They all headed for the dining room. Everyone got busy filling plates and taking seats around the table. Some of the guys filled plates and took them to the front room. Rafe sat at the table holding Dede. Dora sat Lars at the table with the other children. They all grinned at each other. They were enjoying being with other children. They all grabbed up their pizza and started eating.

Rafe told his mother about their visit with Mr. Mills. "Poor man, we should have checked on him. He must be lonely. I think I'll take him a casserole and maybe some carrot cake," she said.

"He will like that. I know he will enjoy having visitors," agreed Dora.

"Have you checked with the school about student teaching this fall?" Madeline asked Dora.

"No, not yet, I have been busy," replied Dora.

"You want to do your student teaching here in Morristown?" asked Mrs. Amory.

"Yes," said Dora, "if they have an opening."

Mrs. Amory took her phone out of her pocket and dialed a number. "Hello, Mildred, this is Mary Amory. Are there any openings for student teachers for the fall?" She looked over at Dora. "She's checking," Mrs. Amory said quietly. She listened in at the phone again and smiled. "Yes, there are." Mrs. Amory turned to Dora. "They have an opening in third grade and one in seventh."

"Third, please," said Dora.

"Yes, Mildred, I have a lovely young woman wanting the third-grade position. Could you put her down for it? Thank you. Her name is Dora Hawthorn. Thanks again. I'll talk to you soon." Mrs. Amory hung up the phone with a pleased expression on her face.

Dora went around the table and gave her a hug.

"You are officially adopted into the family. From now on, everyone, this is Aunt Mary. If it is all right with you?" she asked Mrs. Amory.

Mrs. Amory flushed and smiled. "I cannot think of anything I would like more than being adopted into this lovely family," she said.

Dora gave her another hug and went back around to help some of the children get more food.

Rafe was smiling. Anything keeping Dora close, he was all for.

One of Harry and Ruby's girls got up and came over to Mrs. Amory. "Are you going to be our Aunt Mary?" she asked solemnly.

Mrs. Amory leaned down and gave her a hug. "I would be honored to be your aunt, sweetie," she answered. The little girl hurried back to her seat, smiling happily.

Lars turned toward Dora. "You're going to be my Aunt Dora," he stated. "Jason said so."

All their attention focused on Jason. He just smiled and shrugged his shoulders.

Everyone else got very busy doing other things and ignoring an awkward moment. Rafe just smiled at Dora. "You will if I have anything to say about it," he said to Dora quietly.

Dora smiled at him and squeezed his hand. "We will have this conversation later, without an audience," she answered just as quietly.

When the children finished eating, Maddie took them to wash hands and faces.

"Is Maddie planning on being a teacher, too?" asked Aunt Mary.

"She has not decided yet," said Dora. "She has her senior year of high school to get through first."

"I thought she was fifteen," said Madeline.

"She is fifteen, but she is a year ahead in her classes," said Dora.

"She is following in her sister's footsteps," said Blake, coming into the room for more pizza and catching the last comment.

"She would make a good teacher. She handles the children very well," stated Aunt Mary.

Liam went with Blake back into the front room. Ruby took the baby and went to fix him a bottle. Dora, Rafe holding Dede, Madeline, and Aunt Mary were sitting at the table.

"Mom, Dora and I paid Mrs. Matthews a visit earlier," he said.

"Why would you want to pay that old busybody a visit?" she asked, astonished.

"Dora found out Mrs. Matthews was the one to call in the tip on Harry's children. She called Mrs. Smart at CPS. Well, Dora wanted to be sure there would be no more rumors spread, so she wanted to talk to Mrs. Matthews," he said.

"You know there is no way you can trust a word out of that woman's mouth," declared Madeline.

"Oh, I think she will be quiet about our families from now on," said Rafe with a smile.

'How can you be sure?" Madeline asked.

"Well, Dora not-so-subtle threatened to have her audited by the IRS after making the whole town think her family made its money through selling drugs."

Madeline and Aunt Mary burst out laughing. Dora and Rafe joined them.

"Good for you," said Aunt Mary to Dora. "She has had it coming for a long time."

"Rafe, if you don't bring her into the family, I will," said Jason from the doorway.

"Go find your own girl. Stay away from mine." He reached over and pulled Dora into a hug.

Jason just grinned at him. "Are there any more like you at home?" he asked Dora.

"My older sister is married with two children. Only Maddie is left, and she is spoken for," replied Dora.

"How can she be spoken for? She is only fifteen," said Madeline.

Dora just smiled at her and kept her mouth closed. She had spoken without thinking. She had to be more careful while keeping Maddie's secret.

Everyone finished eating. They put the leftovers away in the refrigerator and threw away the paper plates and cups. Dora smiled with satisfaction when all was clean, and the trash was ready to be taken out. Liam volunteered to take out the trash.

"Do you want this bag taken out, too?" he asked, pointing to the bag by the back door.

"I guess not," said Dora. "I had better wait and see

what happens with Sylvia. The bag is full of her stuff."

"Okay," Liam said with a grin. He took the bag he had outside.

The guys and Maddie took the kids out in the backyard to play. It had a fenced-in play area with swings and slides. There was even a large sandbox and plastic digging tools.

Dora and Madeline were alone in the kitchen. Madeline looked at Dora curiously. "When I talked to Lucy, she did not say anything about Maddie being promised," said Madeline.

"She does not know. I was not supposed to say anything. It just slipped out. We were afraid if the Judge knew Maddie had seen someone in the mirror, he would not let her come to Morristown with me. They would not have been able to go on their cruise. Besides, Maddie knows both have wait until they are older."

"She saw someone here in Morristown?" asked Madeline.

"Yes." Dora nodded.

Madeline thought for a minute. She was thinking about who Maddie could have seen in the mirror. She looked startled as something dawned on her.

"She saw Liam," she said.

Dora looked around before she nodded. "Please don't say anything. She does not want to put any pressure on Liam, with him just starting college and her finishing high school. I should not have said anything. You won't say anything to Liam, will you?"

"I won't say a word until Maddie tells me it is okay," said Madeline. Dora sighed with relief.

Outside the partially open back door, Liam had

been about to come in when he heard his name mentioned. He stopped and listened. Now, he walked back into the backyard with a big grin on his face. He had been attracted to Maddie, but he did not think he had a chance of getting her attention. He smiled. Life sure turned out good sometimes.

CHAPTER 12

*D*ora and Madeline were in the front room sitting and talking. Lars had come inside and over to Dora. He lifted his arms to be held. She hugged him close. He leaned back in her arms and fell asleep. A little while later, Rafe brought a sleepy Dede in and handed her to Madeline.

He smiled when he saw Lars sleeping in Dora's arms.

"Do you want me to lay him down?" he asked.

"No, he is fine," said Dora softly.

Rafe came over and kissed her gently before going back outside.

Madeline just smiled at them fondly.

After Rafe went outside, Jason came in through the back door to get a drink. He came to the front room to drink it.

"Did you get Harry taken care of?" asked Dora.

"Yes, he will be getting some back time starting from when he was hurt. I offered him the choice between working in the office or the cafeteria. He decided to work in the cafeteria. We only serve lunch, so it will be fewer hours, but some people are just not cut out for office work. When he starts work, the head cook lives about a mile from here, so he can pick him up and drop him off. I have made arrangements for him to be examined by a specialist. I want to see if his leg can be helped. He won't start to work until he has seen the doctor." Jason finished his explanation and waited for Dora's response.

"I should have thought about the doctor," said Dora.

"You have been a little busy the last couple of days," Jason excused her with a smile.

Dora smiled back. "Just a little," she agreed. "Thank you, Jason."

"Any time." Jason finished his drink and headed back outside.

Ruby and Harry came in and started to take the girls and Lester upstairs to take a bath and get ready for bed. When the girls saw Dora, they ran over to hug her and say goodnight. She leaned out to hug them so they would not wake Lars. Then Lester approached her shyly to say goodnight. Dora held up an arm to him so he could be hugged, too, then the Wells family all said another goodnight and went upstairs. Harry was carrying the baby, and Ruby had the hands of the two youngest girls.

"You are very good with children," said Madeline.

"I have always loved children. There was never any doubt in my mind about being a teacher," said Dora. "It is what I have always wanted. I could never stand to see children mistreated."

"I know what you mean. When Mrs. Smart from CPS tried to stop us from getting Dede and Lars, I wanted to go up there and pull her bald. Lucky for us, the judge ruled in our favor," said Madeline.

Dora laughed softly so she wouldn't wake Lars. "I do not think Mrs. Smart is going to be a problem for much longer," Dora replied. Madeline looked at her curiously. Dora smiled. "She is on her way out. We just must be sure about the children she removed from their homes. We have to know if it was justified. I just hope the children are not too traumatized."

"You have been busy," observed Madeline.

"Things having to do with children have to be handled quickly," said Dora.

"Yes, they do," agreed Madeline.

Madeline started to get up with Dede in her arms. "I need to get these youngsters home and to bed."

Dora carried Lars and followed her to the door. "Maddie and I are going to have to take the kids shopping as soon as we get some child car seats," she said. "I haven't had time to go shopping for anything."

"We may have some child car seats in the garage. I'll look and let you know," said Madeline. "If they are still there, they are used but still in good shape. At least they were when we stopped using them."

"Great," said Dora. "I'm sure the kids will not mind used car seats. Thank you."

"You are family now. Families help each other." Madeline smiled at Dora. "I am glad you and Maddie are going to be part of our family."

"I am, too," said Dora.

The guys heard them talking and came to the front to see what was going on. "Round up everyone. It is time to head home," said Madeline. Everyone started loading into the van. Rafe came over and took first Dede and then Lars and put them in their seats and buckled them in. He gave them both a kiss on the forehead and told his mother he would be home soon.

"Take your time," she said. "I am sure we can get these two into bed. They are sleeping so soundly; they probably won't even stir."

Rafe put his arm around Dora and watched as they left. Maddie waved back at Liam, who was waving goodbye to her. Blake also waved goodbye.

Then Maddie, Blake, and Jason went inside. Rafe and Dora stayed on the porch. They started to sit in the porch lounger, but Dora turned in Rafe's arms and raised her face for a kiss. Rafe pulled her closer and settled his lips on hers for a long and passionate kiss. Jason started to come outside, but when he saw Rafe and Dora, he turned and went back inside.

After several minutes, Rafe drew back and rested his forehead against Dora's. "I have wanted to do that ever since we met," he whispered.

"Me, too," Dora whispered "Even before we met. When I saw you in the mirror, all I could think about was being in your arms."

"I do not know how the mirror came into existence, but I am so happy it is around. When I think we might not have met without it, well, I just do not want to think about it," said Rafe.

"I think there are a lot of people in agreement with you about that," said Dora.

Rafe started another passionate kiss. They did not even think about sitting on the lounger or anyone else around. They just wanted to be as close as they could be.

After a while, they settled onto the lounger and Rafe leaned back and pulled Dora close in his arms. They sat there, talking softly, getting to know each other. They would chuckle softly when one of them related a humorous incident from their growing up years. Mostly, they just enjoyed being close and touching.

Jason looked out again and, seeing them sitting on the lounger talking, came outside. "I am going to say goodnight," he said to Dora. "Are you going to be in to work tomorrow?" he asked Rafe.

"No, I am going to take a couple more days off," Rafe replied.

"Okay," said Jason. "Goodnight."

"Goodnight," responded Dora and Rafe.

After Jason was gone, Dora looked at Rafe. "I am not complaining, but you don't have to take time off from work. I am not going anywhere. I am settled in. I have a job, and I have you and a whole new family," she said.

"I know. I must go back to work sometime, just not yet. I want to enjoy the newness of seeing you and being with you for a while before getting back into a routine."

Dora smiled and stretched up to give him a kiss. He gladly returned the favor. They stayed on the porch until Blake came out to go up to his apartment for the night.

"Goodnight, you two," he said.

"Goodnight," they responded.

"Has everyone gone to bed?" asked Dora.

"Yes, Maddie just went up. Everyone else was already asleep," said Blake. "You missed a call from Mom and Dad. Dad was not pleased to hear you were outside snuggling with Rafe."

"You did not tell him that," gasped Dora.

Blake laughed. "Relax, I was just teasing. I told him you were upstairs in the shower."

Dora relaxed. "Thanks, Blake."

"Any time. I may need you to give an alibi for me one of these days," he replied as he waved and left, still chuckling.

"I need to go and let you get some sleep," said Rafe. He gave her one more kiss and then pulled her to her feet. He kissed her again and opened the door for her.

"Goodnight," he said. "Lock the door."

Dora gave him one last smile, then closed and locked the door.

CHAPTER 13

The next few days passed quickly. Harry busied himself with small repairs around Hawthorn house after he asked Dora and she gave the okay. Lester was helping him until Aunt Mary decided to tutor him so he would be ready for fifth grade in the fall. Lester was reluctant at first, but he came around when it was explained to him, he would be held back in the fourth if the school tested him when he registered for class. He did not want to be held back, so he agreed to be tutored.

Rafe and his two children spent a lot of time with Dora. Lars had become her shadow. He loved being cuddled. Dede still hung onto Rafe, but she was warming up to Dora. She seemed to be a little jealous of all the attention Lars was receiving.

Madeline sent over two child car seats and one booster seat. Dora and Maddie used them to take Lester and two of his sisters out shopping. They bought all the children night clothes, some play outfits, and sandals. They purchased a stuffed toy and a doll for each of the girls and let Lester pick out some cars for himself. They also bought some noise makers for the baby, who was looking much more alert since he had been receiving his formula. Dora and Maddie had a great time shopping with the children.

The next day, Rafe took Dora to the school so she could fill out the application for student teaching. Mildred in the office was glad to see her and asked how Mrs. Amory was doing. She seemed very fond of her. Dora assured her that Aunt Mary was having the time of her life. Since the children had come, she seemed to have a new lease on life.

One surprise to Dora was how much Liam was hanging around. He was coming by every day and spent most of the time hanging around Maddie. Maddie did not seem to mind. She was always glad to see him and greeted him with a smile.

The Judge checked in with them almost every day. Sometimes Dora talked to him, and sometimes she let Blake or Maddie talk to him. Dora decided to tell him a little about the events in Morristown since they arrived. She did not think he would appreciate being kept in the dark. The next time he called, she was going to catch him up on events. Hopefully he would not jump ship and head home.

They had not heard anything else from the chief of police, so they assumed there was nothing new to report. Blake was going to go by the station just to get an update on the cases.

Dora and Maddie were in the kitchen getting ready to start dinner when Ruby entered the kitchen.

"Hi," she said. "Harry is playing with the baby and the girls, and Lester is with Aunt Mary. I thought I would see if I could help with dinner."

"Sure, we are just making spaghetti and meat sauce. We have the salad makings in the fridge. You can start chopping and mixing them. There is salad dressing in there also. I am going to put some garlic bread in the oven to bake in a little while. We do not want to overcook it," said Dora.

"I want to thank you all for helping us and being so nice to us. We have not had many people be nice to us in a long while," said Ruby.

Maddie came over and gave her a hug. "You are part of our family now. If anyone is not nice to you, you just let me, or Dora know. They won't be able to sit down easy for a while when we get through with them. Nobody messes with our family," said Maddie. "Right, Dora?"

"Absolutely right, Maddie," said Dora with a smile for Ruby.

Dora had been thinking about Mr. Mills. She knew he was lonely and needed repairs done around his house. So, she called Madeline and suggested they all get together and take him food and have the guys work on his house and yard. With a large group, it should not take long to get it all done, and the ladies could feed everyone when they finished.

Madeline thought it was a great idea. She was going to talk to Jason and see if any of the guys on the logging crew would like to help. She said Jason could stop by there and look around, see what needed to be done, and get Mr. Mills's permission. Madeline called back later to let her know Jason stopped by and Mr. Mills gave them permission. They were arranging everything for Saturday.

The ladies got busy deciding what food to take. They were all excited about the picnic, as they called it. Even Aunt Mary was looking forward to the outing.

When Blake went down to the station to check on Sylvia and Derrick, he mentioned the plans to Chief Welldon. The chief and several deputies, who overheard, asked if they could come and help.

"Sure," replied Blake. "The more there, the faster the work will go. I'll just tell the girls to add extra food." Blake left the station smiling. He was still smiling when he conveyed the news to Dora and Maddie later.

"I have been thinking," said Dora. "When Dad calls us tonight, I want to tell him what has been going on. He is going to be very upset if he gets back and we haven't told him anything. At least this way he can be prepared and know what to expect. What do you think?"

She looked enquiringly at Maddie, Blake, and Rafe. Blake looked thoughtful. Maddie looked apprehensive, and Rafe looked supportive.

"I think you are right. He needs time to adjust to everything before he gets back," said Blake.

"You won't tell him everything, will you?" asked Maddie.

"I just want to tell him about the house and his money," remarked Dora. Maddie drew a deep sigh of relief.

"What are you not wanting her to tell?" asked Blake.

"It is not important. It is Maddie's private business," said Dora.

"Okay," said Blake. "Maddie, you know if you need help you can count on me."

"It is nothing like that. I am fine. Thanks Blake," said Maddie.

When the phone rang, Dora took a deep breath and answered it. "Hello, Mom," she said.

"It is not your mom. It is your Dad," answered the Judge.

"Hi, Dad, is Mom okay?"

"She's fine. I sent her on an errand. I just had a feeling you wanted to talk to me," answered the Judge.

'Yes, I do. I wanted to catch you up on what has been going on around here," said Dora.

"I had a feeling I was not getting the whole story," replied the Judge.

"I just did not want to spoil the cruise for Mom. She has been looking forward to it for so long," replied Dora.

"Your mom is having a great time, and so am I. Now, tell me what is happening there," demanded the Judge.

"Well, when Maddie and I arrived, we found out the woman who was cousin Sylvia's nurse had apparently taken up residency in the house after her death. For the past three years, she lived off the money and grocery account you set up for Sylvia. She was selling all the furniture, which we stopped. The police logged the entire thing, and she was arrested. Then Maddie and I went and closed your accounts at the bank and at the grocery. I called Blake to come down and handle Mills and Mills. Blake called the attorney general's office, and they sent someone to look over Derrick Mills accounts. They are issuing a warrant for his arrest."

"Wait a minute," interrupted the Judge. "Derrick Mills? What happened to Albert Mills?"

"Mr. Mills retired because of ill health," said

Dora. "But we checked up on him and filled him in on everything about Derrick so he wouldn't find out on the news or anything. We're going back this weekend with a crew of family and friends to help clean up his yard and fix up the house for him. Derrick hasn't really been helping him keep it up, so it is in pretty bad shape."

The Judge paused for a moment before answering. "Thanks," said the Judge. "I'm glad you went to see him. I am so proud of you and Maddie and Blake. Thank you so much for taking care of my old friend and thank you for letting me know what is going on. The suspense was getting to me. I love you all, and I will see you all at the end of the cruise. Mom and I will come there when we get home."

"We love you, too. We will see you when you get back," said Dora.

Dora hung up the phone and sat back with a huge sigh. She looked over at Rafe, Maddie, and Blake with a grin. "How did I do?" she asked.

"You did great," said Maddie. "I am glad it was you and not me. The Judge can see right through me."

"I think you gave him enough information to keep him on the cruise. He can find out the rest when he gets home," said Blake.

Rafe held her close. "Everything you told him was the truth, just not the whole truth. Promise me you will never play me like that. With us I want everything to be honest and truthful,"

"I promise I will never try to save you from the truth," said Dora.

CHAPTER 14

Saturday dawned bright and clear. Rafe dropped his family off at the Mills home and took the van to pick up Dora and Harry's family. Maddie and Aunt Mary rode with Blake. They put the extra child seats from Dora's car into the van. They even turned one around for the baby. They put most of the food for the picnic into the trunk of Blake's car and were all set to go. Rafe put Dora's hand on the steering wheel and covered it with his hand. Dora smiled at him. This seemed to be his favorite way to drive.

It was a great day for house repairing and yard work. The children could sit in front of the television and watch cartoons. They had Aunt Mary and Albert to keep an eye on them. The women took over the kitchen, and the men got busy outside, with Jason directing everything. He assigned two men, one from the logging crew and one of the police volunteers, to cut grass and trim hedges.

When the neighbors saw all the activity going on, they came over and offered to help. The women brought more food, and the men joined the outside workers. When the women were talking in the kitchen, they said they'd had no idea Mr. Mills was so bad off. They had been meaning to check on him, but with work and family, they just hadn't been over to see him lately. Dora just smiled and welcomed them over. She was hoping this would raise their awareness and they would be better neighbors from now on.

While the majority of the men did the yard work, Jason and Rafe built a ramp for Uncle Albert. It was at one side of his steps and had handrails on each side. When everything else was finished, they were going to paint it with some waterproof paint.

Everyone was having a great time, especially Uncle Albert, as he told the children to call him after hearing them call Mrs. Amory Aunt Mary. He said if she was Aunt Mary, he was Uncle Albert. The children were thrilled to now have a new uncle as well as an aunt.

Dora and Madeline set up a folding table on the front porch. They placed some large jugs of lemonade and iced tea with stacks of paper cups on the table. They put a trash can out there to put the used cups in. They asked Maddie and Rafe's two sisters, Meg and Anna, to sit out by the table and pour drinks for the men, when they came and asked for them. The girls were happy with the task because they got to sit and admire all the guys. Maddie was glad for a chance to get to know Liam's two sisters. They were closer in age to him than his brothers, and she could find out more about his likes and dislikes. The girls were having a great time giggling and talking to each other.

The men working in the yard took every chance they got to stop for a drink and flirt with the girls. The girls just smiled sweetly and filled their glasses. The men were too old for them, but they were enjoying the attention. Dora and Madeline checked occasionally, just to be sure the girls were okay and still had plenty of lemonade and tea. Everything looked fine to them. They were not worried about the men. They knew Jason, Rafe, and Blake would keep them in order.

When the front yard was cut and trimmed, the women asked the men working out front to set up a long table in the front yard. They used a couple of sawhorses and a piece of plywood to make a table. The women covered the table with a sheet. They tied each corner so the sheet would not blow off and started bringing out covered dishes and placing them on the table.

Dora stopped in the front room on her way to the kitchen for more food. She wanted to check on the little ones and make sure Aunt Mary and Uncle Albert were not getting overwhelmed. The children were enthralled with the cartoons and laughing at the silly antics of the cartoon characters. Aunt Mary and Uncle Albert were watching the children fondly and talking quietly to each other. They both seemed to be enjoying some mature company along with the young company. Dora smiled and continued to the kitchen.

"Aunt Mary and Uncle Albert are getting along great with the kids," Dora told Madeline.

"Yes," agreed Madeline. "With each other, also," she added with a smile.

"Yes," agreed Dora.

When all the food was out, along with paper plates, plastic forks, spoons and knives, Madeline called out for everyone to come and eat. The children came pouring out of the house. The ladies started making plates and sitting the kids on the porch to eat. Aunt Mary helped Uncle Albert to walk down the ramp by holding onto his arm.

Uncle Albert looked at his new ramp and beamed. He looked like he was about to cry, he was so happy.

"Thank you," he said, looking around at the men smiling at him.

"You're welcome," said Jason, "but we are not finished yet. We just stopped to eat. We will finish up and paint your ramp."

"I'll never be able to repay your kindness," Uncle Albert said.

"There is no repayment necessary," said Blake. "You are our family. We take care of family." Everyone was nodding in agreement.

"Okay, everyone, let's eat," said Madeline. There was a lightening of atmosphere, and everyone got in line to fill their plates. They were laughing, talking, and having a good time.

Maddie and the girls were still at their table passing out drinks. Liam looked over at them. He did not look pleased to see Maddie surrounded by guys who were laughing and joking with Maddie and his sisters.

Maddie looked over at him and smiled. He did not smile back. He turned around and headed for the food table. Maddie's smile faded. She did not know what she did to upset Liam. No one else noticed how quiet and solemn she became.

After they finished eating, some of the men helped them clean up and take the trash out to be picked up by the trash collector. The remainder of the men went back to finishing up repairs on the house.

Maddie and the girls took the empty lemonade and tea jugs into the kitchen and folded up the table to put away. All the leftover food was put in containers and left in the refrigerator for Uncle Albert to have later.

Madeline volunteered to take Harry and his family home so the younger ones could take a nap. They looked about ready to fall asleep where they were sitting. Each of the children went by and hugged Uncle Albert and told him bye before they left. Madeline assured Dora she would leave the extra car seats on her front porch.

Madeline was only gone about thirty minutes before she was back, ready to load her bunch up and take them home. When she said it was time to go, Dede and Lars both went to Uncle Albert for their hugs. Uncle Albert looked so pleased.

"You will bring them back to see me, won't you?" he asked Madeline.

Madeline came over and gave him a hug also. "You're part of the family now. We will be seeing a lot of you. You will see so much of us, you will probably be wishing for some peace and quiet," she said.

"Not a chance," said Uncle Albert. "All of you will always be welcome in my home."

When Madeline loaded up her kids, Dora noticed Maddie gazing at Liam with an unhappy expression on her face. When he turned to look at her, she quickly turned and looked away. Liam turned and got into the van. He did not look Maddie's way again. He stared straight ahead.

Lars had to come and give Dora a goodbye hug

before they could get him into the van. Rafe brought him over for a hug and then fastened him into his seat. He kissed both Lars and Dede and told them he would be home soon.

"Be good for Grammy," he told them.

"We will," assured Lars. Dede just grinned her sweet grin at him.

The men finished up and painted the ramp while Dora sat in the front room with Aunt Mary, Uncle Albert, and Maddie. The neighbor ladies left after the cleanup was finished. They assured Uncle Albert they would see him soon.

Dora was enjoying tales about her dad when he was young. Maddie was not saying much. She seemed distracted. Dora was worried about her.

When Jason came in and said they were done, Uncle Albert followed them out on the front porch to say goodbye. Aunt Mary held onto his arm.

Blake came up onto the porch and gave Uncle Albert a hug. "Dad said to tell you he would be over to see you as soon as they are back from their cruise," said Blake.

Uncle Albert smiled big and blinked his eyes a couple of times. "If you talk to him, tell him I'm sorry for the mess Derrick made of his accounts," he said.

"He knows you had nothing to do with it. He is just worried about you. He wants to see you and make sure you are all right," said Blake. "We have to go now, but you have our numbers. If you need anything at all, you call us, okay?"

"Thank you," Uncle Albert said.

Blake helped Aunt Mary into his car while Maddie got into the back seat. Dora waved at them and told them she and Rafe would be there soon.

Dora helped Uncle Albert back inside and gave him a hug. Rafe shook his hand, and Dora reminded him to call if he needed anything. They left a happy man inside. He was altogether different from the man they met just a few days before.

When they arrived back at Hawthorn house, Rafe went into the front room to talk with Blake and Harry. Dora spotted Maddie heading for the kitchen and followed. Maddie took one look at Dora and burst into tears. Dora came over and drew her into her arm.

"What's wrong, Maddie?" she asked.

"Liam hates me," she mumbled.

"I'm sure Liam doesn't hate you," said Dora. "What happened?"

"He accused me of flirting with those guys at Uncle Albert's," she said. "I tried to tell him I was only being polite, but he wouldn't listen." Maddie pulled back, and Dora handed her a paper towel to wipe her face with.

"Honey, I'm sure Liam doesn't hate you. He is just jealous. He does not know you very well. You are both very young. He is probably having feelings he doesn't know how to deal with, so he lashed out at you. He is probably feeling as bad as you right about now. Just give him some time to think about things. He will come around."

"Maybe you are right, but why does life have to be so complicated?" asked Maddie.

"I guess life wants to keep us on our toes," Dora said with a laugh.

"Yeah," agreed Maddie. They started to leave the kitchen. They did not see Rafe hurriedly head back to the front room. He had been looking for Dora and had hung back when he heard Maddie crying and

Dora talking to her. He had not wanted to intrude. He was going to have a talk with his little brother. It was not acceptable for him to make Maddie cry, no matter what his excuse. Even if he was jealous, he did not get to take it out on Maddie.

CHAPTER 15

*M*addie went to her room to lie down for a while and let her puffy eyes fade. She did not want the others to know she had been crying. Dora joined the guys in the front room. She smiled at Rafe and started to sit by him on the sofa, but he stood up and took her hand. She looked at him enquiringly. "Let's sit on the porch for a while," he suggested. Dora smilingly agreed and turned and led the way outside.

They sat on the swing, and Rafe put his arm around her and pulled her close to his side. "I was wondering about something," he said.

"What?" Dora asked.

"Did Maddie see Liam in the mirror?" he asked.

Dora nodded reluctantly. "Yes, but please don't tell him. She doesn't want him or anyone else to know. They are both so young. She did not want him to feel obligated to her. We did not even tell our parents. We were afraid they would not let Maddie come with me this summer if they knew. The only other person aside from me and Maddie to know is your mom, and she guessed. You won't tell him, will you?" Dora looked at him pleadingly.

"I will not tell him, but how did she see him in the mirror?" asked Rafe.

"It was the last time we saw each other in the mirror. Remember, you were in your bedroom and Liam was with you. The two of you were talking. I was surprised when Maddie could see you. No one else has been able to. Then, I realized it was Liam she was seeing. I had her step back so Liam would not see her, and he left the room. You saw her looking around the mirror, but she could not see you anymore."

"I'm glad you told me. I will not say anything about it. I want you to know you can tell me anything. I don't want there to be any secrets between us." Rafe kissed her gently. "I love you, and I want us to build a life together. I want you to know you can trust me. When are your parents going to be home from their cruise?" asked Rafe.

"They have two more weeks. They are coming here when they return," said Dora.

"Good, I am going to have to make a good impression on the Judge so he will give me permission to marry his daughter," said Rafe.

"You might want to ask his daughter first. She may not say 'yes.'" Dora smiled mischievously.

Rafe pulled her closer in his arms and kissed her passionately. "You are mine," he said, "just as I am yours. You are going to say 'yes,' aren't you?"

Dora kissed him again. "Oh, yes," she sighed.

Rafe left shortly afterward, after a nice make-out session. He said goodnight and got Dora's agreement to go to church with him the next day.

Dora went inside, said goodnight to Blake and

floated upstairs to prepare for bed and dream of a life with Rafe, Dede and Lars, and all the rest of the Haggerty family.

When Rafe arrived home, he found Liam sitting on the front porch steps. Rafe went over and sat down beside him. They sat quietly for a few minutes, looking up at the stars. Liam looked over at Rafe several times. He seemed to want to say something but didn't quite know what to say.

"How do you know when you find the girl meant for you?" asked Liam.

"You just feel it inside," responded Rafe. "It doesn't always work out. Sometimes the girl doesn't feel the same way as you do. You have to get to know her and let her get to know you."

Liam sighed. "I think I have messed up. I doubt she will ever speak to me again."

"You have to be careful in the way you talk to anyone. Especially girls, you can hurt their feelings easily. When I was at Hawthorn house, Dora was comforting Maddie. Maddie had her feelings hurt by someone and was convinced the person hated her. She was very upset. She didn't even join the rest of us, but went straight to her room," Rafe said quietly.

Liam looked upset hearing about Maddie crying. He bowed his head and looked at the ground. He did not say anything else. Rafe gave him a lot to think about. When his jealousy struck, he struck out. He was sorry Maddie was in the line of fire. He was going to have to see her tomorrow. If she would talk to him, he was going to have to apologize to her and hope she would forgive him.

Liam said goodnight to Rafe and went inside. Rafe sat for a few minutes more. He had wanted to let

Liam know he'd made a mistake without breaking Dora's confidence. Rafe went in to check on Dede and Lars before going to bed.

Both children were sound asleep. Rafe kissed their foreheads and straightened their covers. He then went to his bedroom. When he reached his room, he took out his phone and called Dora.

"Hello," said Dora.

"Hi," said Rafe quietly. "I just wanted to tell you goodnight one more time and tell you I love you."

"I love you, too. I'm glad you called. I missed you from the minute you left," Dora sighed.

"How soon can we be married? I want you with me all of the time. I do not like having to leave you," said Rafe.

"It is not going to be easy. We have to wait until Mom and Dad get home, and then the wedding will have to be in Rolling Fork. Uncle Ralph will have to be invited, and I'll have to check on his schedule. Bobby Larroue will have to be invited, so I'll have to see when he can come."

"Bobby Larroue, the race car driver?" asked Rafe.

"Yes, he is a friend of Dad's. He is also Maddie's godfather. He would be very upset if he was not invited," Dora responded, smiling at Rafe's excitement. It was not unusual for them to receive visits from Bobby. The Judge and Bobby were good friends. Bobby always tried to come by on Maddie's birthday. When Dora was thirteen and Maddie was eight, Bobby had been working on his car at their place while he was visiting. Blake was eighteen at the time. All three of them had watched while he worked on his car.

Bobby had decided to give them a few pointers on

fixing a car. He taught them how to change a tire, how to do a tune-up and check belts and fluid levels. He showed them how to do minor repairs and keep a car running long enough to get expert advice, if it was needed. At first, their mom was upset when they all came in with grease on their hands and faces, but when she saw how much fun they were having, she withdrew her objection and learned how to change a tire herself.

They had not had to use their knowledge of a car's working yet. But when Bobby visited, he would check to be sure they remembered what he'd taught them. They were all happy to prove their knowledge to him.

"Is there anyone else we have to invite?" asked Rafe.

"Yes, but they can work around our schedule," said Dora.

Rafe laughed. "We'll work it out. I cannot believe Bobby Larroue is going to be at our wedding. Jason and Liam are going to be so excited. So are Meg and Anna. Even Mom will be excited. I love you. One thing I know for sure, life with you will never be boring. I will see you in the morning. Goodnight."

"Goodnight," said Dora.

Rafe arrived to pick up Dora for church the next morning. He brought Dede and Lars, strapped in their car seats, with him. Dora had to lean into the back seat and give Lars a hug and kiss. Then, Dede decided she wanted to be hugged, too. So, Dora hugged her and let Rafe open her door and seat her in the front seat.

Rafe and Dora both smiled with satisfaction at

Dede's action. Everything was working out fine for their family.

When they arrived at church, Rafe carried Dede in. Lars showed his independence by walking beside Dora and holding her hand. Rafe led the way down the aisle and seated them all in the row with his mom and his sisters. Liam and Jason were seated in the row across the aisle. As friends and neighbors came in, they stopped briefly to say good morning. Dora was surprised at how quiet and well-behaved Dede and Lars were.

After church, they all went back to Rafe's house, where they were joined by Maddie, Blake, and Harry's family. Madeline had lunch all prepared and invited some friends to join them. Except for Maddie and Liam, they were a big, noisy, happy bunch.

Maddie was ignoring Liam. Every time he tried to get her attention, she pretended he did not exist. He finally cornered her on the back porch. She had taken a bag of trash out, and Liam seized his chance to talk to her. She started to walk past him without acknowledging him, but Liam reached out a hand to her.

"Maddie, please, I'm sorry. I had no right to talk to you like I did. I'm an ass. If you will forgive me, I promise I will never do it again," he pleaded.

Maddie looked at him hard for a minute. Then there was the trace of a smile at the corner of her mouth. "I'll forgive you this time, but I will not be called names by anyone. I learned to take care of myself at a very young age. I will wipe the floor with you if you treat me like that again. You caught me by surprise this time. I did not expect such behavior from you. It will not happen again."

Liam smiled at her. "So long as you talk to me and smile at me, I don't care if you wipe the floor with me," he assured her.

Maddie burst out laughing, and Liam joined her. They both went inside to see what else they could do to help.

Rafe and Dora were glad to see the two of them enter together, smiling. They returned to seeing Dede and Lars served with lunch before fixing their own plates.

The next two weeks were passing quickly for some, more slowly for others. Dora and Maddie started giving self-defense lessons to Meg and Anna each morning. Some of the younger children would watch and imitate them, so Dora took them aside and gave them pointers, too.

They gave the lessons in the front yard at Hawthorn house. At the end of each lesson, they were surprised to discover a crowd gathered, watching with interest. They did not know if the watchers were more interested in the lessons or the pretty girls in exercise outfits. The girls ignored the crowd and got down to the serious business of learning to defend themselves.

Harry had his doctor's appointment. Jason and Ruby went with him. Dora and Maddie volunteered to watch the children so Ruby could go along.

The doctor said he was going to have to reset his leg. It would have to be broken and reset so it would heal properly. He would be off work for about two months. They took him back and did the work without waiting. He would have to stay overnight so he could be monitored.

Dora assured Ruby the children would be fine if

she wanted to stay with him. Ruby was hesitant asking them to watch after such a number of children overnight, but Dora calmed her and told her they would be fine.

The next morning, Aunt Mary asked Dora if she could talk to her in the kitchen. She seemed nervous. Dora smiled at her and tried to calm her. "Is there some problem I can help you with?" asked Dora.

"No, dear, I want you to know how happy I have been, staying with you and your lovely family," said Aunt Mary.

"It has been a pleasure to get to know you, too," replied Dora. "We all love having you here."

"It is just...Albert is so alone. He has asked me to move into his house. We love spending time together, and if we are together neither of us will have to worry about being alone as we grow older." Aunt Mary paused and looked at Dora.

"I think it is a wonderful idea. I have been worried about Uncle Albert. Even if you are at his house, we can still visit. I know the children are not going to give up their Aunt Mary and Uncle Albert. You are part of our family now. When did you want to move in with Uncle Albert?"

"I already have most of my things packed. I just have to load them in my car, and I will be ready to go," said Aunt Mary.

"Let me get Blake to load and handle the lifting. He can follow you over and help you unload. We do not want you to hurt yourself." Dora called out for Blake, and he came from the front room to see what was going on. He was glad to help and followed Aunt Mary to her room to start taking things out. Maddie soon was helping also.

When the children heard Aunt Mary was leaving, the girls started to cry. Dora gathered them around and assured them Aunt Mary was not going far. She was going to be at Uncle Albert's. They would get to see both often. They stopped crying and went to hug Aunt Mary.

"We love you," they told her.

"I love all of you," she told them all, including Lester. "I promise we will see lots of each other." She gave them each another hug and then found some small things for them to take out to the car so they could help.

They all stood out front and waved Aunt Mary goodbye. After she was gone, Dora ushered the children in and sat them down at the table to eat.

Dora and Maddie decided to move Harry and Ruby and the baby into Aunt Mary's room so Harry would not have to manage the stairs with his crutches. Dora left Maddie feeding the children and went to change bed linens. She would have Blake move the cradle when he returned.

CHAPTER 16

The day finally arrived for the Judge and Lucy to return from their cruise. Blake, Maddie, and Dora were all anxiously awaiting their return. Lucy called them when they disembarked. As soon as they claimed their luggage, they started the drive to Morristown. It would take them about three and a half hours to arrive.

Maddie and Dora cleaned Harry and Ruby's old room and got it ready for the Judge and Lucy. They changed a small office downstairs and turned it into a bedroom for Lester. Dora and Maddie set about arranging a meal for the family. They fixed some of the dishes they knew their mom and dad was partial to.

When their parents arrived, all three of them hurried outside to greet them. After lots of hugs and excited chatter, Lucy, Maddie, and Dora went inside, leaving Blake and the Judge to bring in the luggage. After showing their mom where their bedroom was and giving a quick tour of the upstairs, they headed for the kitchen to start putting the food on the table.

The Judge looked at the little girls and Lester, and

then he looked at Dora. "I think you left out a few details in our talk," he said.

"Dad," she said, pointing at Harry and Ruby. "This is Harry and Ruby Wells. These are their children. Uncle Ralph gave me custody of them so I could help them. Harry will be able to go back to work with Jason Haggerty when his leg heals; until then, we are helping them out."

The Judge went over and shook hands with Harry and Ruby. "If Dora says you need to be here, I know she will take good care of you. You are all welcome at Hawthorn house."

"Thank you," replied Harry. "Your family has been great to us, especially Dora. I don't know what would have happened to us without her help."

"Yes, I am very proud of all of my family," replied the Judge.

They were just sitting down to eat when the doorbell rang.

"I'll get it," said Dora. She knew it would be Rafe. She had told him when the Judge and Lucy were coming in and expected him to arrive at any time. Dora opened the door and went into his arms and raised her face for a kiss. The Judge investigated the hall and saw Dora in Rafe's arms. He sighed with resignation and went back into the dining room.

When he went over to Lucy, she patted his hand and smiled. "They all grow up, dear," she said.

"I know, I was expecting it, but the reality is still hard to accept," he said.

Rafe and Dora came into the dining room, holding hands. "Dad, this is Rafe Haggerty," said Dora.

Rafe held out his hand to the Judge. The Judge

shook his hand and smiled. "Hello, Sir, it is a pleasure to meet you. I am in love with your daughter, and I have asked her to marry me. She said 'yes.' We hope to have your blessing."

The Judge did not say anything for a minute. He wanted to see if Rafe would squirm. Rafe waited calmly. "I have known since Dora saw you in the mirror that you were going to be a part of our family. I trust my daughter implicitly. So, I am pleased to give you my blessing." The Judge held out his hand to Rafe. He then pulled Dora into a hug, and Lucy came around and hugged Rafe then Dora. It was a happy bunch gathered around the table.

Blake filled him in all the happenings with Albert. He told him about Sylvia and Derrick and how their cases were advancing. Dora and Maddie were busy chatting with their Mom about plans for Dora and Rafe's upcoming wedding.

They finished eating and cleaning up when Madeline and the rest of the family came. Madeline and Lucy were very happy to see each other. They hugged each other and started chatting a mile a minute.

Jason, the girls, and Liam were very interested in meeting the Judge. Dede and Lars headed for Rafe and Dora. Dora scooped Lars into her arms and cuddled him close. Rafe gathered Dede into his arms. The Judge looked at Dora holding Lars, and he smiled with a softened expression on his face. He came over and rubbed a hand gently on Lars's head.

"Well, young man, are you ready to meet your new granddad?" he asked.

Lars peeked up at him, and then he smiled big and held up his arms to the Judge. The Judge took him in his arms and cuddled him. Lars looked happily satisfied.

Dora looked at Rafe and smiled. Everything was going to be just fine. Dora was very glad she had answered Love's Call.

The End

ABOUT THE AUTHOR

Betty McLain

With five children, ten grandchildren and six great-grandchildren, I have a very busy life, but reading and writing have always been a very large and enjoyable part of my life. I have been writing since I was very young. I kept notebooks with my stories in them private. I didn't share them with anyone. They were all handwritten because I was unable to type. We lived in the country, and I had to do most of my writing at night. My days were busy helping with my brothers and sister. I also helped Mom with the garden and canning food for our family. Even though I was tired, I still managed to get my thoughts down on paper at night.

When I married and began raising my family, I continued writing my stories while helping my children through school and into their own lives and families. My sister was the only one to read my stories. She was very encouraging. When my youngest daughter started college, I decided to go to college myself. I had taken my GED at an earlier date and only had to take a class to pass my college entrance tests. I passed with flying colors and even managed to get a partial scholarship. I took computer classes to learn typing. The English and literature classes helped me to polish my stories.

I found public speaking was not for me. I was much more comfortable with the written word but researching and writing the speeches was helpful. I could use information to build a story. I still managed to put my own spin on the essays.

I finished college with an associate degree and a 3.4 GPA. I had several awards, including President's List, Dean's List, and Faculty List. The school experience helped me gain more confidence in my writing. I want to thank my English teacher in college for giving me more confidence in my writing by telling me that I had a good imagination. She said I told an interesting story. My daughter, who is a very good writer and has books of her own published, convinced me to have some of my stories published. She self-published them for me. The first time I held one of my books in my hands and looked at my name on it as author, I was so proud. They were very well received. This was encouragement enough to convince me to continue writing and publishing. I have been building my library of books written by Betty McLain since then. I also wrote and illustrated several children's books.

Being able to type my stories opened a whole new world for me. Having access to a computer helped me to look up anything I needed to know and expanded my ability to keep writing my books. Joining Facebook and making friends all over the world expanded my outlook considerably. I was able to understand many different lifestyles and incorporate them in my ideas.

I have heard the saying, "Watch out what you say, and don't make the writer mad, you may end up in a book being eliminated." It is true. All of life is there to stimulate your imagination. It is fun to sit and think about how a thought can be changed to develop a story and to watch the story develop and come alive in your mind. When I get started, the stories almost write themselves; I just have to get all of it down as I think it before it is gone.

I love knowing the stories I have written are being read and enjoyed by others. It is awe-inspiring to look at the books and think, "I wrote that."

I look forward to many more years of putting my stories out there and hope the people reading my books are looking forward to reading them as much.

Love's Call
ISBN: 978-4-86751-752-9
Mass Market

Published by
Next Chapter
1-60-20 Minami-Otsuka
170-0005 Toshima-Ku, Tokyo
+818035793528

9th July 2021